Hope ...

Anyway

Moving Day ...

1.

Lisa L. Walsh

Hope ...
Anyway

Lisa L. Walsh

ZIMBELL HOUSE
PUBLISHING
UNION LAKE, MICHIGAN

For permission requests, write to the publisher:
"Attention: Permissions Coordinator"
Zimbell House Publishing
PO Box 1172
Union Lake, Michigan 48387
mail to: info@zimbellhousepublishing.com

© 2018 Lisa L. Walsh

Published in the United States by Zimbell House Publishing
http://www.ZimbellHousePublishing.com
All Rights Reserved

Print ISBN: 978-1-947210-43-1
Kindle ISBN: 978-1-947210-44-8
Digital ISBN: 978-1-947210-45-5
Library of Congress Control Number: 2018904665

First Edition: June 2018
10 9 8 7 6 5 4 3 2 1

ZIMBELL HOUSE PUBLISHING
UNION LAKE

Dedication

To my brother Andrew.

So grateful to have shared so much of my journey
with you.

Contents

Prologue

"I'm not going in that house, and you can't make me!" I slammed the door that Mama left open and settled into the seat, crossing my arms tightly across my chest. Mama, who had waited for me on the porch, shook her head and went into the house, without me. *Finally.*

There is great safety in being stubborn. It can be like a giant, comfy cocoon. Just ask Sam-I-Am's friend. He had no desire to eat those nasty green eggs and ham. I totally get that. I wouldn't have either, not today or not tomorrow. Not in a van or with a tan. I find it to be a great tragedy that Sam-I-Am's friend finally gave in and ate that green gook. He lost my respect, then and there. If I were there, I'd have put my arm around his shoulder and told him to stay strong. And I'd have told Sam-I-Am to get lost. As for me, I'm keeping my stubborn. It's strong, and I'm glad.

What's this all about? Well, guess who's in there, inside of that sprawling, beautiful, off-white Cape Cod style house with the two big dormer windows? Mama, Bean, and Jerry. My not-so-smart family, that's who.

I can just picture them, strolling around the spacious rooms with the new, plush white carpet and freshly painted walls. Did I mention there's a separate laundry room? Who needs that?

They're looking at details, soaking it in, trying to look like they fit inside of those starched walls. The hoot of it all? That place belongs to a rich family. They act like we might someday live there. I say, *Get Real.*

And me? I have taken refuge in the great safety of Mama's bumble bee yellow Dodge Colt, we call Buzz, parked on the curb of Evergreen Drive. I'm just shaking my head in disbelief at the whole idea.

I have refused to budge from Buzz. I refuse to pretend that I'm going to live there someday. Not me. The nicest house I've ever lived in was a moved-in-from-the-country, about two Taylor Swift songs away from being torn down farmhouse. When people see my house, they'll say, "Poor Heidi. She has it so rough." That farmhouse cost two-thousand dollars. For the whole thing. I'm not ashamed to say that. Now we can't even afford that.

I bet my whole life, people will say that about the place I live in. It's okay. I don't mind. I may be only fourteen—almost—but I know about getting your hopes up.

The main thing is that life just isn't easy, and you'll probably not really ever get what you want. Especially underdogs like us. I wish my family would stop fooling themselves; stop playing games.

I feel kind of sorry for them actually. Getting your hopes up just makes it all that much harder when the truth catches up to your dreams. And doesn't it always? I'll keep my scabs securely attached, thank you very much.

Recently, at my Monday night Alateen meeting, our sponsor Mike said it's okay to want things for yourself, to tell yourself you're worth it.

Okay, Mike. I want to move into the Schluter mansion on Main Street in Graceford, Illinois. Should I start packing?

I've been down this road before—well, not Evergreen Drive exactly—and I'm not letting myself hope.

I expect them to be back any minute, probably all dreamy-eyed and scramble-brained. And then we can get back to real life. At least I will. Scabs in place. The rest of my family, well don't be surprised if they're just a little bloody. Serves them right.

When it comes to a life, if anyone tries to tell you that they have the whole story, about anyone, they are wrong. Sure, every earthly life has a physical beginning and a physical end. But none has a real, true beginning or true end. Birth and death are important, but they aren't the bookends. Our stories wrap around each other, one weaving in and out of another, like each individual strand of hair in a braid. A new birth may be the beginning of a new person on a birth certificate, or 'it's a girl' or 'it's a boy' sort of way. But no baby comes into the world without connections to parents who have histories and experiences. We all have a story.

It's sort of like a photo. You can get a really good feel for what's happening at the split second when the shutter is opened, but you don't know what voices were there or who might have been standing just outside the border.

But, then again, a photo doesn't have to be complete to be beautiful. I think that's my point.

I'm about to tell the story of Bean and me, Bean who is in that sprawling house with Mama and that Cowboy-Hippy Jerry. Then maybe it will make sense why I'm out here in Buzz, and Bean and the others are in there, volunteering for a punch to the heart.

Our story is really a giant mix of said and unsaid stories. But I'm going to search for the guts. There is beauty in the middle, and I'm going to try to find that creamy filling. You know the creamy center? It's the very best part.

Chapter One

A Fresh Start

Heidi's favorite beginnings:

1. Mine, beginning on my own birthday.
2. Bean's, one year and one week before mine.
3. The first day of summer vacation.
4. The first chocolate chip cookie about five minutes after coming out of the oven.
5. Wearing brand new shoes.

The first person I noticed when Bean and I were ushered into the eighth-grade classroom at Graceford Grade School was Simone Schluter. She was sitting, front and center, posture perfect, her deep brown hair brushed so that it moved as one piece, like a waterfall. Hand under her chin, she sported a great big smile for her two new classmates.

"Can she sit next to me, Mr. Verbrecht?" she asked in a saccharine voice, both eyes and teeth gleaming. Then she glanced to her seat neighbor and gave her just the slightest raise of an eyebrow.

Her seat neighbor quietly giggled. There was no room next to Simone.

I decided right there that Simone could be trouble.

My brother and I found two empty seats toward the back of the classroom. I lowered my head as I walked down the aisle, but in order to see where I was going, I looked up just in time to see a sweet, friendly smile. A girl with long, wavy hair and smiling deep brown eyes gave me a little wave and motioned with her thumb to the empty seat next to her. I gave her a little smile back and then slid into my desk.

"Hey, pal," the smiling girl leaned toward my desk, speaking softly. "We start with English class." She then faced back to the front.

Thank you, I thought, and I took a breath maybe for the first time since I had entered the room.

It was early October, and the school year was well underway. Mama had finally decided that she was leaving our Daddy, Frank A. Walker, for good. We had been on our own in Evanston for at least six months. Daddy, who was absent more than he was present, had been gone too long. Mama filed for divorce, and finally decided that she, Bean, and I would move to tiny Graceford, about three hours south. Mama's hometown. Before, it was the place we came to know through holidays and week-long vacations. Now, we would call it home.

I loved my daddy. But I was not sad that he was gone. Mama was my anchor. I often pictured her during the early years of their marriage as a young lady, feet firmly planted on the ground. In her hand was a string. At the end of the string was a kite; a beautiful, colorful kite that flew high in the air. Mama sure loved that kite, but it was far away. Daddy was the kite at the end of that string. The wind blew that kite round and round. I never understood where that wind came from. But it was strong.

After he lost a job, Daddy would be gone for sometimes days and sometimes weeks at a time. Mama would say, "Nobody but me understands him." But eventually, she realized she needed to open her hand and let the string go, love it or not.

So, she did. And the three of us came to Graceford. The Walker Trio.

When we entered our apartment above the Graceford Bank, I wanted to love it. In fact, I was determined to, but there was no doubt about it. It was really, really tiny.

"I know it's small, but we won't be here for too long. I've got to save up some money. I just need to get my first paycheck. I already have plans in the works for a cute little house." Mama was trying to make all of us feel a little better. Including herself.

"It won't take long." Mama had been hired to be a work supervisor in a rehabilitation center for disabled adults; brain injuries, mostly. She was excited about her new job.

Mama and I would get one bedroom, and my brother Jeffery, known to me as Bean, would get the small one. For a while, it had been hard to say who was going to get their own room; Bean or Mama.

I just knew for sure that it wouldn't be me.

As tiny as it was, I didn't mind. I was thrilled the three of us would be together. And free of Daddy.

"How far is it to Grandma Baker's house from here?" I asked while we took our clothes out of the totes and put them into the dresser drawers. I propped Harey, my bunny with the silky ears my Uncle Billy had given me on my fifth birthday, against the bed pillows. I never sleep without Harey. I'm not sure I even could.

"Five minutes," was Mama's answer.

Five minutes from Grandma Baker's house. I couldn't believe it. "Wait. Walking or driving?"

"Walking. It takes a minute to drive there."

Five things to know about Grandma Baker's House:

1. Her doorbell. It rings to the tune of "Hit the Road, Jack." She thinks it's hysterical.
2. There's a Bible in every room.
3. Uncle Billy can only practice his guitar from ten am to seven pm.
4. Smells like cinnamon rolls all the time—*Yummy!*
5. If she offers you food, take it. She'll get mad if you don't.

Grandma Baker, Mama's mother, lives in a small, red brick gingerbread-looking bungalow tucked away on Morningside Court, on the edge of Graceford. It's one of the coziest homes you've ever seen and one where some sort of music always lives. Either through her own beautiful voice or something low in the background on her music player.

Grandma is a gardener. She can grow nearly anything. In the summer, the flowerpots below her windows are brimming with bright, colorful blooms and long, hanging vines in varied colors of green.

During the holidays, she puts boughs of pine in the boxes, and at night, lights of all colors glimmer brightly from them. Her porch wraps around the east side, with more plants and flowers displayed all around. On the porch, we sit in big white wooden rocking chairs to watch the sunset.

Grandma Baker loves beautiful things.

Uncle Billy lives with her. It's just the two of them.

My Uncle Billy, Mama's much younger brother, has always been one of my very biggest fans, and I am his. When we visited from Evanston, he would spend lots of time with me, doing whatever I wanted. I liked to play Princess when I was little, and I would assign Billy the role of the Evil Queen. He relished it. Eventually, he even somehow obtained an Evil Queen outfit just for such occasions. "You're the evil queen," I'd say. Billy would cackle wickedly, disappear for a moment, and return in a stunning purple iridescent dress and headpiece unashamedly.

All for me.

Billy always made me feel special.

A few weeks after we arrived in Graceford, Addy, my little cousin, and I walked to Grandma Baker's after school.

While we walked, a grown woman walked by us, looking disheveled and talking to her baby doll. I tried not to stare at her when she went past, and when she was out of earshot, I asked Addy who she was.

"That's Mrs. V. I don't know her real name."

"Is she a crazy?" I asked my little cousin.

"Na. Mommy says she's just different."

Different. Seemed like a better way to put it.

It was a Thursday, and on Thursdays, we had what Grandma Baker called a 'permanent date.' Until Christmastime anyway. The three of us were going to complete a handmade advent calendar together.

On this particular Thursday, we had completed six of the twenty-five ornaments for the Advent calendar when Uncle Billy, a senior in high school, snuck through the kitchen door and tried to avoid his mom.

"Going somewhere, William?" Grandma said, killing his plan. "The school called today. Mind telling me where you went after lunch? You do understand that you can't just leave school?" she asked, sewing a beaded black eye on a Christmas penguin, maybe a bit too aggressively.

Billy stuck his head around the corner, careful not to make eye contact with Grandma. "Hey, Mighty Heidi. Hey, Addy Able." He headed to his room; no greeting for Grandma. The slamming door shook the living room.

"Don't have children," she said to us, laying her sewing supplies in her lap and cupping her squinched face in her hands.

Addy and I, wondering if Grandma knew she just wished away our existence, looked at each other with surprise.

Though I loved just walking to her house, with my cousin, no less, there was always some sort of drama with Uncle Billy. I wished Billy would stop getting in trouble, but I also really thought Grandma was mean to him.

Grandma did know how to needle someone. Uncle Billy calls it nagging. When she needles me about Mama, it's a little hard to take.

"Heidi, what time did your mom make it home from work? Did she make you dinner?" These were the kinds of questions I would have to answer.

What really surprised me were the nasty things she would say about Daddy, and how her comments made me angry. "Heard from that no-good Pa of yours, Heidi? I can't believe Frank hasn't scheduled a visit with you and Jeffery lately. Something's really wrong with that man ..."

Somehow, she made the word 'pa' a cuss word, I just didn't think it was necessary. And though she didn't call me no-good, it sure felt like she did.

But none of that would keep me from going to one of my very favorite places on earth. Remember the cinnamon roll smell? And if Uncle Billy was home and everyone in a good mood, that would just be a bonus.

"I can't wait for the game to start," Grandma said, practically giddy. "I think the Cubs just might do it this year."

"Do what?" I asked honestly.

"Win the World Series, Heidi."

"Did they win last year?" I was serious.

"Last year? Heidi, they haven't won since 1908."

A voice carried down the hallway, "Do you remember it well?" Billy asked his Mom.

"Very funny, William. Very funny."

Grandma Baker was a Chicago Cubs fan. When we moved to Graceford, the Cubs were in the M.L.B. playoffs, and some were saying that they might win. I was at Grandma's during one of the games against the Dodgers, watching while we sewed more ornaments for the calendar. Inning by inning, I got more interested in this team. Baseball was fun—who knew?

Uncle Billy watched, too, usually wearing a Cubs jersey with a big '23' on the back. Some old player named somebody Sandberg, I guess.

Addy, poor kid, wasn't allowed to stay for the games, which were on pretty late. That was the excuse that Aunt Nettie and Uncle Toad gave. But I knew the real reason. Uncle Toad was a Cleveland Indian fan. Indians. Now there's another word, *Indians*, that Grandma Baker can't say without spitting it out as quick as possible.

A Walker Trio Extra: Favorite Stories

Me: Pots and Pans

Mrs. Wilkerson said, "Good morning girls and boys. Who would like to share a little about your weekend?"

This question came from my first-grade teacher on a Monday morning and was how we started our day pretty much every Monday. Many of us raised our hands—students giving typical examples such as movies, family picnics, and birthday parties. I was excited to finally have a report; sometimes life at our house was plain boring. Finally, Mrs. Wilkerson called on me.

Mrs. W.: "So Heidi, how about you?"

Me: "My dad got in trouble by the cops for hiding pots and pans."

Mrs. W., her facial features squeezed together toward the middle of her face, "In trouble? For pots and pans, Heidi?"

Me: "Uh-huh. Well, Daddy called Mama to say that when he got pulled over, the cops looked under his seat and found pots and pans. Then Daddy spent the night in jail."

Mrs. W., whisking me into the hallway to have a private conversation, "You might not want to tell the whole class if your dad gets arrested, Heidi."

Me: "Are pots and pans bad, Mrs. Wilkerson?"

Mrs. W., "I'll let you ask when we call your mom at recess."

Bean: Bubble Lights

He's a mad scientist, Bean. And I, unfortunately, am his long-time and semi-retired lab assistant.

When we were about three and four, Mama bought bubble lights for our Christmas tree. You know the ones; a glass ball with a tube at the end that contains a liquid that bubbles? They're really old-fashioned. Like so many things Christmas, our tree looked dazzling. Magical. Tasty? Bean thought so.

He convinced me that the liquid was some sort of magic juice. "Would it make us fly? Take us to the North Pole?" I was so naïve. When Mama took a nap, we plunged them in, biting the ends off of those glass ornaments—you see the problem here—draining the contents. I broke only one and was sorely disappointed to find basically no taste to this magic liquid whatsoever. But my misplaced optimism, taken directly from Bean, lead me to hope the sugary flavor lay on the bottom of the bulb.

Needless to say, Mama was furious with us, and had to contact her person at the Poison Control Center. Again. Bleach. Aspirin. Birth control pills. Everything had to be locked away. Bean was as relentless as I was loyal.

Mama: Cops are Coming

The time that I was most proud of Mama? Not long before we moved to Graceford, we were in the car, and Mama was driving through Evanston to pay a power bill.

Something caught her eye. "Hold on, Heidi," she said calmly as she jerked the wheel and turned the car around. She drove, fast, up to some random house, and I saw a man whom I had never seen before choke-holding a woman whom I had also never seen before. Mama evenly said, "I'll be right back. Stay here."

I rolled my window down to hear what was going on. My heart pounded.

Mama stepped right up to the man and shoved her finger into his face. In a strong, steady, and loud voice she explained, "Listen, asshole. You get your hands off my friend here, get in your car, and drive away. Now. I've called the cops. They're on their way."

The man scampered away quickly. The woman went in her house, and Mama returned to the car, put it in drive, and we drove off.

"Mama?" I asked. "Who was that?"

"I have no idea," Mama answered. And that is the last she ever said about it.

Chapter Two

A Real Home

What to Know About Graceford Grade School (with a lot of help from Madari Swinford):

1. You are a Graceford insider if you were born in Champaign County.
2. You are an outsider if the above does not apply to you.
3. People know your family's business, often before you do. Want to know what's going on in Graceford? With your own kin? Check with Nosy Norma Sampson.
4. Mr. Verbrecht, the eighth-grade teacher, is the best teacher ever! Rumor has it that he makes tasty treats all the time in science— his favorite—class. Just stay on his good side.
5. We're about to live in the newest old house in Graceford!

Things were really tight in our little upstairs storefront apartment, and not long after our Graceford adventure began, Mama said we were in for a treat. We were moving into a real house. Bean and I had only ever lived in apartments.

Bean and I were celebrities for a day as Mama saved a small farmhouse that was to be demolished and moved it into the town on wheels. The price? $2,000. Now that seemed like a lot of money to me, but when adults heard that we bought our house for that amount, they would act astounded.

"Two-thousand dollars? For a house? Oh, Joy, that is unbelievable," grownups would nearly gush.

The whole school came out to the front schoolyard mid-morning as the house was wheeled through Graceford, heading to the empty spot at 110 South Walnut Street.

Bean and I fielded questions from every direction.

"Which is your room, Heidi?"

"Will it have cracks all the way through?"

"Will they be moving the basement, too?"

"How will it stick to the ground?"

"Are the sink and toilet still working while the house moves on the road?"

Even Simone Schluter showed some rare interest. "That house was my aunt and uncle's before they built their brand new one. It has only one bedroom."

"Where are you all going to sleep?"

I, of course, knew the answers to very few of these questions, except that the one bedroom was going to be mine. But I loved that my classmates asked. I felt 'a part' instead of 'apart.' It was pretty cozy on the inside of that circle. But I knew it wouldn't last.

My bright spot was Madari Swinford.

"Hey pal, you saving this seat?" she asked on my first day of school at lunch. Bean and I were together, but there was space right next to me.

"For you, pal," I answered back, and we were off.

Madari, born in India, had long wavy black hair and beautiful dark eyes. The Swinfords, her adoptive family, wanted her to be called Madison, but she liked the name Madari, and so did I. Madari and I became close, a friendship bonded mostly through being underdogs. I tried to remember to call her Madison when I was at her house, but I usually forgot. Only to be corrected by her mother or father.

"Look, I'll never be one of the Graceford originals," Madari said when we were in her room one day after school. "I wasn't born here. I look different." She shrugged. "Suits me fine. To be a Graceford original means to be mean. A few years ago, they started to call me names, like Jungle Girl. I pretended like I liked it."

"Liked it? Did you?"

"Of course not. But I wouldn't give them the satisfaction of knowing that. I actually thanked them. That stopped it."

I laughed. I couldn't imagine thanking someone for being nasty to me. I'd have to think about that one.

Bean bonded quickly with Tommy Milton. Tommy moved a few years earlier from Galena, a town in northwest Illinois, but never really felt accepted either. Tall and bold, Tommy demanded attention. The four of us became our own team of sorts, standing outside of the tight circle of insiders, and grateful not to be alone.

At the lunch table on the day before Halloween, the four of us were finalizing our plans for trick or treating. We decided that, as eighth-graders, it would probably be the last time we would don costumes and beg for candy, and there was no question that we would go together. We would dress as hobos. It was the cheapest and easiest costume.

"I'm a professional Halloween hobo, I have dressed as one so many times," Bean announced proudly.

"Ha! That's so funny," Madari's laugh was like a song. "A professional hobo. Hey! Like, that's an oxymoron."

"Hide, tell them about your 'gypsy' costume? It's the best!"

"Oh, yeah! So, my Mom dressed me as a gypsy, in a flowy skirt and head scarf. Picture this little tiny girl, standing in the front of the class."

"Pretty easy to do, Heidi. Have you grown at all?"

"Very funny, Tommy. So, I was in the front of the class, and I couldn't think of the name of my costume, so I panicked and told everyone I was a 'hooker.'"

Suddenly Simone started banging her spoon on her tray, stopping my friends mid-laugh.

"Listen everybody. Listen!" The whole cafeteria grew quiet. "Let's go trick or treating as a class! All of us!" Simone announced at the lunch table, looking, for some odd reason, at me. "We'll meet at my house. And Heidi, is it okay if we *all* dress like hobos. It sounds like so much fun!"

Our group looked at each other, more than a little surprised. The others shrugged, and I spoke for the group.

"Um, okay, sure," I said. "Why not? Six o'clock at your house."

"Yeah," she said, and with each of the next words, she clapped. "It's (clap). Going (clap). To (clap). Be (clap). So (clap). Great (clap)!"

Something about the way she clapped made my stomach drop.

The next day, Madari and I rushed to her house after school and got ready. We planned to step it up a notch, and dress as Zombie Tourist Hobos, complete with loose and falling dried glue on our faces, cameras around our necks, oversized shoes, and pillows under our Hawaiian shirts. We agreed that we looked pretty great.

We met up with Tommy and Bean, who had gotten ready at Tommy's, about a quarter to six, and headed to Simone's big house on Main Street. Every window on every floor was lit up with jack-o-lanterns. The front porch was aglow with purple and orange lights.

"I'm not so sure about this," Bean said when we reached the door.

Before I could answer, Simone swung the door open.

"Happy Halloween, friends! Come in!"

Simone was certainly no hobo. She was dressed as a perky butterfly ballerina, complete with a short, wide, fluffy tutu, sparkly wings, and lively antennae. Behind her stood several of our female classmates; a perky bumble bee, a perky ladybug, a perky cat, a perky bunny, and a perky skunk smiling at us behind their perfectly made-up faces.

Shouldn't Simone have been the skunk? I asked myself. The tightness of the glue was starting to seriously itch.

"Can I take your, ah, your cameras?" Simone's mother asked. We clutched them tightly. "Did you see the girls' costumes? Aren't they just darling? Simone came up with the idea for them all by herself. And what are you girls supposed to be? Dead clowns? How very, ah, brave."

Six boys from our class, all dressed as their favorite professional sports heroes, stood in an uncomfortable clump toward the back of the room, looking straight at the ground. They held caramel apples and studied the carpet.

We stood there in stunned silence, Madari and I, our glue faces falling off.

"Six boys and six girls? Look, I think this is supposed to be, like, a date," Madari finally said to me, quietly. A strand of glue dangled from her chin, swinging back and forth.

"And we've been treated to a trick," I punched at my own stomach pillow. "We're the show."

Bean jerked his head and thumb toward the door, and without a word, the four of us turned and walked out. We hit the street, a little wiser, to gather candy on our own. We knew the rest of the collective eighth-grade gang would not be looking for us. Their point was made, at least Simone's was. I felt like a fool.

I apologized to the group for bringing them to Simone's.

"Hey, don't worry about it, Hide," Bean offered. "They're the ones who made fools of themselves. I seriously doubt that they will even have any fun. Besides, they would just slow us down."

Which was true. We hustled from house to house, gaining serious speed and collecting sweet treasures, trying to leave the shadow of the perky creatures far behind.

Madari, in a half-jog, was the only one who complained about the pace.

"Look pallies, you may be more fun. But would you please slow down?"

A few days after Halloween, the Chicago Cubs were battling the Cleveland Indians for the World Series title. One month ago, I barely knew a Chicago Cub from a Los Angeles Dodger.

I learned fast.

The afternoon of November 2, I finished my homework early and packed up an overnight bag. I was going to watch the Cubs finish this season, either winning it all or going down in flames, with Grandma Baker and Uncle Billy. Of course, I had convinced myself that Harey was a Cubs fan, too. I swore once, when the Indians took the lead, Harey's silky ear covered his eyes. I think Harey cared. He really did.

Uncle Billy couldn't take it. He was in and out of the room twice an inning. Once the Cubs lost the lead, and the game went into a rain delay, Billy flew out the front door into the night. He just couldn't watch. Or not with us, anyway. Once, I spotted him peeking through the living room window.

But the Cubs pulled it off, and Billy's heart fully recovered. Even though it was after eleven on a school night, we celebrated by jumping up and down. Grandma even broke down and cried, which was strange, I thought, for a game. But when I thought about this being something that she waited for her whole life, it made some sense. We slept in the living room, where we watched history made. The Cubs. World Series Champions.

As I made my way about Graceford, which was slowly becoming a new normal for me, I kept seeing Mrs. V., the grown woman walking around town and talking to herself or her doll. For some reason, spottings of Mrs. V. were important. It was an announcement from the world somehow, saying 'Look here, Heidi! Things could always be much worse!'

Mrs. V. was known simply as the crazy lady. She had three daughters, the oldest was one year older than me with wildish brown hair, and the younger two, twins I think, were simply adorable little girls with blonde braids and dirt-smeared faces. If you tried to talk to Mrs. V., which Bean and I did—be friendly to everyone, our mother's words echoed in our heads—she would not answer you outright, but her volume rose. If her daughters walked with her, they refused to make eye contact.

I felt sorry for them, I really did. But I felt something else, too. Something small and ugly, but I couldn't really put my finger on it. Let me just say I kept my eyes open for them.

In November, we moved from our upstairs storefront apartment to our famous, at least by Graceford standards, little farmhouse smack dab in the middle of town. Fresh paint, sanded hardwood floors, it was a cute little home. The prettiest features were the two windows in the front, a big picture window in the front room, and the small dormer window from my room.

Mama, Bean, Uncle Billy, and I set to painting the house. The kitchen was a bright white, and my room, which had a pitched ceiling and a window looking out over the town, was painted a pale but cheery yellow.

Grandma crocheted me a grey throw blanket with the biggest yarn I had ever seen. I wrapped myself in it every night.

Our new home was not fancy by any means, but it was sure respectable. Bean's room had no privacy; it was basically the loft at the top of the stairs. My room was just beyond his—one had to go through his room to get to mine.

Mama had a big room down in the basement.

Our first night there, I walked from room to room; soaking it in. My favorite was my very own room. It was my safe place. I felt a little guilty that Bean didn't have any privacy. But he didn't complain, and I didn't offer to share.

Our own house. This place, all prettied up and new, in its own way, was just as good a setting as any for a family to fall to pieces. But who knows that on the first steps of a new journey?

A Walker Trio Extra: Important Facts

Me: Bean and I are in the same class because I was part of an experiment at Northwestern University in the town of Evanston, where we lived until October of our eighth-grade year. A research project from the education department was looking to determine the ideal age to start school, and when I was four, they were looking for four-year old's through six-year old's to begin kindergarten. Mama signed me up.

They continued to track our progress through fifth grade. I have no idea what they found, but every year, we would be observed and interviewed. What it meant for me, though, was that I was always the smallest and youngest in my class. And when we moved to Graceford, it also meant that Bean and I would be in the same class as there was only one class per grade. A lot of people think we are twins.

Bean: When he was born two months early to our still teenage parents, his doctor referred to him as undercooked. The doctor told my mom that he would probably struggle in school. But Bean is smart and has an insatiable curiosity. I wouldn't be surprised if, hearing what that doctor said while swaddled up against Mama's chest, little baby Bean squinted his little right eye, raised his left eyebrow, and said inside his newly formed and wired brain, "I'll show him!"

Mama: Mama, like Bean, was super smart in school. When she was young, she wanted to be a pediatric oncologist. She would have been a good one, too. She's not grossed out by things like blood, poop, or vomit.

Grandma Baker says that her interest in boys grew bigger than her interest in school once she got to high school. Part of me thinks that is a shame, because she would have been a great doctor. The other part, though, is glad. Because if she hadn't been so interested in boys, I wouldn't be here.

Chapter Three

The Unexpected Graces of Graceford

More About Bean:

1. He has used the words 'justice' and 'inequity' for fourteen days in a row.
2. Bean may not stay on Mr. Verbrecht's good side. My brother likes to argue.
3. His sense of direction is terrible! He gets lost in Graceford all the time!
4. His table manners are not improving.
5. Bean seems to be completely immune to the normal eighth-grade desire to be popular. (See #4)

On the first Saturday afternoon after moving in, Bean and I decided to explore the neighborhood. Now Graceford is a small town. It is basically two one-mile streets and one half-mile street, running north and south, with several small east-west streets connecting them. If your address was Graceford, you probably lived on Main Street, Park Street, or the smaller Walnut Street. From space, it probably looks like two and a half ladders.

There isn't much to do in Graceford. There is a gas station, a bank, and a couple of bars. No grocery stores, no restaurants. A good imagination is necessary in order to have fun.

We had never had much reason to be on Walnut Street, but now that we called it home, we wasted no time in becoming familiar with it. We ended up hiking down the railroad tracks heading west of town. The railroad tracks were on the far north side of our property.

What we found was nearly magic. After about a five or six-minute walk, which took us past sugar gum trees that boasted bright orange, red, and yellow leaves, we came across a tangle of vine-like trees, grabbing and holding each other, making what seemed to be a large room. It was late autumn; some leaves had fallen.

Bean and I entered the fort, standing on the thick and colorful rug of leaves. The domed top split the sky into puzzle pieces.

"Hide, this is amazing. What kind of trees do you think these are? They might be some sort of aspens?" Bean wondered aloud.

"Beats me."

After a few minutes of walking around, we sat on a couple of large stumps toward the center of the fort. I started thinking about being here, both in Graceford and in this particular space. It occurred to me that, at this moment, our world was full of people whose lives were about to change. For some, tragedy was waiting, and they had no idea. And for others, some of whom wouldn't expect it, good was just ahead. A stroke of luck. The moment they had been waiting for. Life certainly was full of surprises.

I mean, who would have guessed a year ago that we would be here, living in Graceford. Then I looked at my brother, in this new place, and wondered where we were in our journey. I saw something that was, anymore, rare on his ever-thinking face. It looked like peace. It had been a while since I had seen that.

"Hey, Bean. How are you?" I asked for maybe the first time. Our lives had been spinning and churning for a while, and for the first time that I could think of, it felt like we had stopped. The ground was steady.

Especially here.

He started to say something smart, then looked at me. I was serious.

He picked up a leaf and examined it, smelled it. "I'm fine." He cracked a small corner off and started to chew on it.

"I mean it. How are you?" I kept my gaze steady.

He looked at me then, paused for a moment, and then shrugged. "I don't know, really. How are you?" He spit out the leaf and sampled another.

"I think," I started, "Well, I think I am pretty okay. I'm ready for things to stop changing, to dig into where I'm at."

Once I began, I started to talk. Really talk, like a tight ball of string loosening and unraveling. I told him that I was relieved to be leaving Daddy in the rearview mirror, and that I was so glad to have our happy mom back. I told him that living so close to Grandma and Uncle Billy and Aunt Nettie's family sometimes felt like a dream. I told him that I felt like I may not ever make a lot of friends at school. I could tell Bean all of these things because who was he going to tell? Nobody. And he had been through it all, he just saw it all from a slightly different angle. We lived it together. We had just never really talked about it.

Bean listened, and my words poured out.

I guess it was contagious.

Bean's voice got really soft when he started talking about Daddy. He missed him and felt like a piece of him was gone now. I remember when Daddy would come back after being gone for weeks at a time. Bean wouldn't take his eyes off him, like if he did, Daddy would disappear again. Poof. My brother tried so hard to keep Daddy close. Bean needed Daddy like I needed Mama. And now, he was gone. He talked about visiting him, and how he looked forward to that. Bean also talked about feeling like an outsider at school, but he thought kids were more accepting of him than me. He didn't know why, but he didn't like it.

We ran out of words, falling into a comfortable silence as the sun started to sink toward the horizon, we were not in this alone.

We were pretty okay.

We were also naïve.

I thought I understood. Mama had a job, a new house, no more broken promises. She had a lighter spirit than I had ever known. Mama's hair, which she had cut a few years before, had gotten long again, and was so golden, she really looked like a child herself. It wasn't uncommon for people to ask if she was our older sister. I thought the joy was shared and had to do with this new life that we were building. The three of us. The Walker Trio.

But the missing piece? The real reason for Joy Walker's newfound happiness?

His name was Jerry.

A Walker Trio Extra: Looks

Me: When I look at myself, sometimes I think I look a little cute. Other times, I think I might be a real live actual mouse. Only in human form.

Hair: Brown, medium long. Medium thick. Looks best in a braid or two braids, French or otherwise.

Nose: completely different from Mama's and Bean's. My nose is flipped up at the end. My nostrils may be the first thing people notice about me. It's a little cartoonish. Like how a five-year-old might draw a nose. Round with two holes.

Teeth: Too big, stick out a little, with a little chip on the edge of the inside of the front right tooth. I have to talk around them. I'm not getting braces. At least until I can afford them myself. But I do pretend to have braces sometimes; I use aluminum foil.

Eyes: Big. Light blue, like the edge of the sky.

Bean: When I look at Bean, the word interesting comes to mind. Sometimes I think, Hmm, I don't think he's as ugly as he used to be. Bean was born with a lopsided head that resembled the shape of a bean. That's how he got his nickname. Sometimes girls say he's cute, but that is taking things way too far.

Hair: Blonde, and usually floppy. Especially when he runs.

Teeth: Quite huge, and reaching out for you, like they want to grab something. Or bite you. Better since he got braces.

Nose: Long and not so elegant.

Eyes: Light blue, like the edge of the sky.

Mama: When I look at Mama, I think she is the prettiest lady on the planet. Her hair is a golden yellow. For as far back as I could remember, her hair was long. When I was ten, she came home one Saturday, and her hair was cut short with lots of layers. I hated it! I didn't talk to her for a week. It's grown back, now. Mama looks softer with her hair long.

Teeth: Bigger than the average front teeth, but nice and straight. I dare you to look away when she smiles. You can't.

Nose: Long and elegant.

Eyes: light blue, like the edge of the sky.

Chapter Four

Jerry Roadhouse

Jerry Roadhouse was a giant mix between hippy and cowboy, with shoulder length curly brown hair and unnaturally tanned skin. He lived in Graceford and drove a gray, trashed out pick-up truck. The worst news for me was that Jerry used to date my mother back in high school. He knew Mama before I did. For some reason, this fact really kicked at my heart.

"He's only a friend," Mama would say. "He just wants to help us out," she reasoned when Jerry was spending way too many nights and weekends around what had finally been our perfect little family.

Grandma and I shared suspicions about this Jerry character, and his intentions, from the very start. In fact, when she figured out that Jerry and Mama were together, she sat Mama down and asked why she would hook her wagon to that train wreck again.

To which Jerry, who OF COURSE was with Mama, replied, "Because this wagon can sure make your little girl feel good." Then he looked steady into Grandma's eyes until she turned a strange pink color and marched out of her own living room.

I followed, stomping in Grandma's footsteps. Our anger, our disgust, was one.

"That fellow is bad news. Your mother doesn't need a man," my Grandma said, kneading dough for rolls that she would bake in the morning.

"All she needs is us, Grandma. She even has her own job!" I knew Grandma would like me saying this and would agree. I even tried to make my voice like hers when she was on a roll about something. I wanted to serve her up something that she would absolutely agree with.

Bean and I first met Jerry on a Friday night in early November.

Mama, long hair in braids, smiled sweetly at us just before leaving for work that Friday morning. "I'll have a real nice surprise for you when I get home."

"Maybe it will be a cute little beagle puppy," I hoped out loud as Bean and I walked to school that morning. Bean said he would be happy with a pizza.

After surviving an especially long day of school, I swear math class itself lasted five hours, we watched out our front window all afternoon, anticipating the sight of Mama's car.

Buzz rolled into the dirt driveway as the sun was setting and the sky was a misty purple. What I noticed first was that Mama wasn't driving her car. A curly-headed man with a seriously goofy smile was. They got out of Mama's car and met, standing way too close, at the driver's side headlight. He was holding one of Mama braids in his hand. It was a terrible sight, but I couldn't tear my eyes away. *Is this some horrible joke? Is this unwelcome stranger the surprise Mama told us about?*

The front door opened, and the tall man with the ridiculous curls falling around his face and a clown smile stuck on it, held his hand straight out. *At least he took his hand off my Mama,* I thought.

"Jerry Roadhouse. So pleased to meet you. Your pretty mother has told me so much about both of you."

Bean clapped his hand in Jerry's. My poor brother looked like a sucker in a bad business deal.

"Funny, Mama never mentioned your name," I said clearly, channeling Grandma Baker's sharp tongue. My head was on fire.

Jerry's eyebrows shot up on his cowboy-hippy forehead. Mama, in turn, shot me an angry look. I then shot straight out the door and down the tracks to the fort, where I took out my notepad. In the deep and soft purple light, I could barely see. I scratched out my latest list anyway.

Things I hate about him:

1. His stupid mustache.
2. His greasy curls.
3. His stupid little giggle.
4. He is a bad, really super bad, TERRIBLE surprise.
5. His hands on my Mama. She is *MINE*.

I slammed down my pen. My blood boiled. *Does my mother really think this is going to be a good thing? How?* I sat in the fort while the world and my mood turned darker.

Not long after I finished writing, Bean poked his head between two trees.

"He may not be that bad, Hide. Give him a chance."

"Never," I said. "Never. We are going to be ruined again. I just want it to be the three of us."

Bean held out a bag of lemon drops. "He gave us these."

I'd never let him know that those were my favorites. I'd never eat them.

I slapped them away, the bag making a solid crunch on the leaves.

I may have been just twelve years old, but I knew bribery when I saw it.

Jerry may not have won me over, but he sure did Mama. Just like that, they were attached at the seams. Since he started snaking around, I just about never saw Mama without Jerry, usually with a hand on her shoulder or around her waist, or something gross like that. He couldn't keep his lips off her.

I had a big problem with Jerry right from the start. He looked like he was going to steal my Mama right out from under my nose. Mister 'He's Only a Friend' doesn't bring candy to the kids without a real secret reason. Mister 'He's Only a Friend' doesn't sneak out of your mom's bedroom in the morning, claiming to be fixing the sump pump.

One day after school, while working on our Advent calendar, Grandma asked me if I had seen Jerry around before we moved to Graceford. "Did he ever visit you in Evanston?" Grandma needled. For some reason, everything about this question made my hair stand on end.

"No! I never saw him in my life. Not until Mama introduced him as the world's worst surprise."

"Hmm," is all Grandma said. But deep down I knew what she was getting at. She suspected that Mama and Jerry were together, or at least planning on being together, before we even moved here.

I thought about asking Mama when I got home. But then I thought about something Uncle Billy said to me.

Once, when we were talking about who Billy's dad was, he said he had some ideas.

"There are a few possibilities."

"Why don't you ask?" I asked him.

"Heidi. Don't ask a question you don't want the answer to," Billy answered.

So, I didn't ask. Because I didn't want to know about Mama and Jerry.

The following weekend, early Saturday morning, I heard a call from downstairs.

"Get your rubber boots, kids! Rusty leaves at nine am sharp!" Jerry yelled up the stairs. We would quickly learn that when Jerry said we were leaving at nine, it really meant we were leaving at 8:55. He meant the wheels would be rolling on the road at nine.

For us, this was new.

"Where we going?" Bean yelled downstairs. Neither of us were stirring yet.

Here came Jerry's little giggle. "With any luck, we're going to see a baby llama born today."

I walked into Bean's room and yelled over the stairs.

"Do I have to go, Mama?"

I heard a little whispering, and then Mama's voice. "Yes, Heidi. We're all going. Billy, too."

"I don't want to." Actually, I did want to. And was secretly pleased that Billy was coming, too. But the fighter in me needed to make a point.

After Bean headed down the stairs, I went to his sock drawer and lifted a pair of socks, went in my room, and got dressed.

I had been, to be honest, stealing Bean's socks for ages. Bean is a bit of a sock genius. We are always behind on laundry. Always. But what seems to be at all times, Bean has clean socks, neatly rolled together, facing the same way, in his sock drawer.

I don't even have a sock drawer.

So, when I need socks, I just go get his. For the longest time, I thought he didn't notice.

Then, the summer of 2015, he knocked on my bedroom door, entered like a royal herald, and made this announcement:

"As of today, June 14, 2015, you owe me $48.23 for wearing my socks. $3.92 is interest."

Not even looking up for my reaction, he turned and walked out. I boiled.

This practice continued. He never said a word to me about it other than his quarterly reports. I continued to wear his socks, and he continued to charge me. With interest. And the weasel refused to tell me his rates.

At 8:55 a.m., we poured ourselves into Rusty and Jerry drove to a big, sprawling farm about a half an hour away, to a county I had never even heard of before. Vermilion County? Who knew?

There were animals running around everywhere; chickens and cats and goats, and llamas. This couple didn't have any kids, so Bean, Billy and I sort of were on our own. We spent a lot of time chasing around playful little kittens in a shed.

One kitten, all black, followed me around wherever I went. It would climb up my leg and 'mew' at me until I picked it up. It was magically soft and magically sweet.

We went into the barn, my little furry friend underfoot. We found each couple sitting on a hay bale, each grown-up with a bottle of beer in hand. I figured Mama was doing her old trick; someone would offer her a beer, and she would just hold onto it.

Then she brought the bottle to her lips and took a big drink.

"Let's go find the llamas," I said to Bean and Uncle Billy. I didn't come here to see this.

With Jerry around more and more, things began to change. As much as it cramps me up to say so, some of these changes weren't so terrible. All my life, it seemed that Daddy wanted to keep Mama, Bean, and me stashed away somewhere. He didn't feel comfortable around others, including family. We pretty much stayed to ourselves. Mama would joke about it.

"You're just being paranoid, Frank," she would say softly with a little laugh at the end. But still, probably to avoid conflict, we would keep to ourselves, waiting for Daddy to come home from wherever it was he went.

But Jerry, he was a meeter and a greeter, and talker and a partier. He even seemed to like to be around Mama's family, which is funny, because my Grandma said the meanest things about him when he wasn't around. But to his face, she was almost always nice. Mostly. I could read her face though. My Grandma Baker had a sharp tongue. She could say what sounded like the nicest thing, but a few of us knew that she was really cutting you to shreds. "Jerry, doesn't your hair look nice today?"

Jerry would hitch up his jeans, looking quite pleased with himself. Which is super interesting, because what she really meant was, "Jerry, how about those balls of turds on your head?" Eventually, though, the nice act ended.

I spent time with Grandma Baker because she made me feel useful and she taught me all sorts of things. That fall, I learned how to fry chicken, make a meatloaf, bake an angel food cake, crochet a scarf, prune a rose bush. Grandma was always busy with something and would teach me, acting like I was doing her a favor. I soaked it in.

With it, I would listen to her talk about her friends and family. When she got negative about people, I would generally change the subject, or sometimes even bring up something that Pastor Jim said in church. But when she talked about Jerry, I let her roll and often joined in.

"Do you know that he's got Mama drinking now?" I told her the week after the llama farm visit, where we never did see any llama born, like Jerry promised.

Grandma didn't respond right away, which was unusual. She continued to push her needle in and out of the gold fringe around the large, rectangular material that would hold the Advent calendar ornaments.

"I'm going to tell you something, Heidi. Men will change you. Your mother is a smart, capable woman. She does not need Jerry Roadhouse." She went back to her sewing. "She already has everything she needs. And if she's not careful, she's going to lose that."

Though I didn't really understand all of Grandma's words, I felt like they were true. And I felt like we were a team. Still, I wished I hadn't told her about Mama's drinking.

So, because of Jerry the cowboy-hippy, we got to spend more time with the family. In the beginning, Mama's brother Billy, now eighteen years old, thought Jerry was surely a second cousin to God, and worshipped him. Jerry would let Billy borrow his pick-up truck, and would throw in a quarter tank of gas and a six-pack to get Billy and his friends where they needed to go. Can you guess what Grandma Baker thought of that? She was angry.

Secretly, though, I loved that Jerry wanted Billy around. So, did Bean and Mama.

I think being around us was good for Billy as well. At age nine, he was diagnosed with Type One Diabetes. And in his teen years, he wasn't doing a great job of taking his insulin or watching his eating, which is what you need to do to keep it under control. His eyes were starting to fail, and sometimes his feet would go numb. He and Grandma Baker had lots of fights.

I understood that Grandma was worried about his health. I understood that she was afraid he was not going to graduate from Adamsboro High School next May.

"William!" she yelled sternly after she ended her call from the high school. I could tell she was prepared to rip into him.

"Why don't you just tell Billy you're scared?" I asked.

Grandma looked at me for a long time. I was afraid I had said something really bad, the way she stared. Then she closed her eyes, let out a big puff of air, and held out her arms for me to climb in.

"I'll try it," she promised as we held each other.

Mama nagged Billy a little, as it was easier to take from his big sister.

Billy always tells me he is going to die young, and he's going to have fun while he's here. I try my best not to think about that. I can't stand the thought of this world without my Uncle Billy in it.

We were always heading off on some adventure. Now we're headed to a llama farm, now we're going to help some complete strangers move, now we're celebrating someone getting married, today, we're going to celebrate someone getting divorced. If a town within a sixty-mile radius was having a celebration, as long as Jesus wasn't on the guest list, we were there. Life was one big party for Mama and Jerry, and Bean, I, and sometimes Uncle Billy, were usually along for the ride. It was exhausting. It was also invigorating if I'm forced to tell all the truth.

Eight-year-old Newt, Jerry's son who spent every other weekend with us, was often alongside as well. Newt was absolutely as shell-shocked as Jeffery and me at this union that our parents seemed to be forging, and he too was dragged along to these crazy adventures.

Newt was a quiet kid. His best tricks were knowing all the words to every commercial ever written and obtaining and saving money. You would think these tricks would come in handy every so often. But it's not often that you need the commercial lyrics at a moment's notice, and he wouldn't give up a dime of that money of his if you tried to pry it out of his hot little hand. We tried, Bean and I, we really did. Newt had a grip.

Daddy, of course, was not a big fan of Mr. Jerry. They had history. Mama, Jerry, and Daddy were all in the same grade in high school. And Mama dated both of them. Rumor has it that the majority of their bonding time happened at Wednesday after school detention.

We visited Daddy every few weeks, nothing regular, and Daddy asked what seemed like hundreds of questions about Jerry. Then he would get quiet and moody. It was weird to spend time with Daddy in this way. At best, Daddy seemed to me like an assistant parent. When we lived in Evanston, he was never in charge of us, and didn't really know how to be. Driving to his apartment on our visits, he would ask us things like, "Do you guys want supper tonight?" or "Did you happen to bring toilet paper?" Did he think we would not need toilet paper? Was he serious?

One Saturday, Daddy took us home to our little town farmhouse. I knew what was going to happen as soon as I saw Jerry in the yard, stacking wood in preparation for a big bonfire.

Before we could stop Daddy, he marched right out to where Jerry was stacking wood. Now Jerry didn't and doesn't know a stranger or feel the need for any enemies.

"Frank, hey! Geez, long time, no see! Wow, you're looking real goo—"

Before he could finish his sentence, Daddy answered with a punch right to the face. Daddy wrestled Jerry down, spitting curse words and talking crazy. Fortunately for Jerry, soon after the one-sided brawl began, a smackdown, really, the County Sheriff happened to drive by and aimed for law and order, calling out their names from the moment he emerged from the squad car.

In a matter of a minute, he stopped the fight and sent Daddy on his way. He told our Daddy he was no longer welcome in Graceford, which I figured was going to clear our weekend schedule for a while.

Later that night, at the bonfire, I made note that Mama drank a few beers. Which was starting to be too common. Until Jerry had come along, Daddy was the only drinker in our family. And we saw where that got him.

The next morning, I looked out the little dormer window of my bedroom just in time to see Mrs. V. walking alone. The small and ugly feeling was stronger and began to take shape. Sightings of Mrs. V. fed something in me that was hungry to see something bad happening for someone else.

Her pain somehow lessened the tight ball of anger that was building inside about my life.

Just like that, Daddy was gone. That was more okay with me than it was with Jeffery, who seemed to be trying to please an invisible Daddy even when we had no idea in the world where our real Daddy was. Even I began to miss him. That kite was flying further and further into the sky.

"They're just jealous because their lives are so boring," Madari said, trying to protect me the following Monday at school. We were waiting outside by the bleachers at the start of P.E. class. I appreciated her attempt, I really did, but I knew why they were talking.

"It might have something to do with the fact that we are a train wreck. The Greatest Show on Earth," I half-heartedly laughed out my misery as I stretched my calves. It felt like everyone was whispering about Daddy and Jerry's fight; I saw pity in their eyes. I couldn't help but think we were nothing but entertainment for our fellow Graceford neighbors.

Madari stretched her arm out over her head. "Ah, don't let it get to you. None of us lives a perfect life."

I agreed with that. But, still. How many of our classmates saw their dad taking out their mom's cowboy-hippy boyfriend in their front yard for the whole world to see?

"Come closer, class. Gather in," said Ms. Mac, our P.E. teacher, signaling for our wayward class to join her at the bleachers. She was explaining the details of the Pop-Tart mile. I learned that the whole junior high did this every year. And for motivation? The winners won a six-pack of cherry or brown sugar Pop-Tarts. Winners' choice.

We were the last class to run. The times to beat? 6:52 for the boys, 7:19 for the girls.

Bean raised his hand. Without words, I tried to get him to put his hand down. I could tell by the look in his eyes that whatever it was he wanted to say wasn't a good idea. He paid no attention.

Madari sidled up beside me and whispered, "Look, let's not let Simone win. She did last year and wouldn't stop bragging about it. She ate her cherry Pop-Tart *at* me. You understand? *At* me! Get her, Heidi."

"Wait, what? Me?" I immediately started compiling a list in my head. "First, what makes you think I can beat Simone? At anything. Second, I don't need any more reason for her to hate me—"

"Okay, pal, just forget it. Scaredy Cat." Madari leaned way to her right and stretched her hip. "We'll all suffer."

I looked at my friend, feeling annoyed. Now, why did Madari think that I could, or that I wanted to win? Why would I want to put that kind of pressure on myself, winner of the Pop-Tart mile? Then people might expect me to, I don't know, be good at something. My brain reached back to the play we did for English class, when we performed, just for ourselves, Tom Sawyer. I practiced the lines for Becky Thatcher for days and felt so disappointed when Simone got the part instead. I got the part of Mary, Tom's cousin. That scab was still crusty, and it still stung. I wasn't looking for another one.

Finally, Ms. Mac called on Bean, whose arm had to be cramping. Before he spoke, he cleared his throat. "Have you given much thought to the fact that you are asking us to run a mile, which will burn calories, and then rewarding the winner by giving them, basically, a block of sugar? Isn't that defeating the whole point of fitness, Ms. Mac? I wonder if you'd consider giving a bag of carrots?"

The class groaned, and Ms. Mac offered Bean a smile that never reached her eyes and a half-hearted thanks for his concern.

Then we were back to business.

"Okay, boys and girls. Line up even with home plate. See the cones? It's a big area. That far cone is a little hard to see." Here she pointed to a far area of the school property that I had never noticed. "You will run around the marked area two times. That's exactly one mile. When you cross the playground a second time, I'll be reading out times. Go write yours on the clipboard on the bleachers. And no cheating! You'll get an F!"

We lined up. I was, out of nowhere, excited. I'd never thought of myself as super-fast, but I knew that I could keep running. I realized, standing at the starting line, that I really wanted to try to win this Pop-Tart mile.

"Aaand, Gooo!" Ms. Mac shouted, chopping her arm through the air. And we were off. Running out past the baseball diamond, I reminded myself to stay steady. I knew not to use all my energy at once. By the time we were on the backstretch, a handful of my classmates were ahead of me, Simone and some boys. Most were breathing hard and ragged.

Across the playground, I passed Simone.

"You're going to run out of energy, Heidi," she said as I went by.

Bean was out front, but before I knew it, I had taken over second place.

"Three minutes and thirty seconds, thirty-one, thirty-two," Ms. Mac shouted as I passed for the first lap. "Great job, Heidi! Keep it up!" I heard the excitement in her voice, and it immediately turned to fuel.

"Good, Simone, Three thirty-eight, nine, forty. Strong run!" She was behind me, and I wasn't going to let her win. My lungs were burning, and my breath was coming fast, but my focus was on one thought, *I'm not going to let her win.*

I steadied my eyes on Bean, who was churning out a good pace, his hair flopping up and down. I figured Simone was close, but I didn't look. I just concentrated on moving my legs. I even picked it up a little in the back half of the lap, through the playground, charging the finish line.

"Six fifty-four," Ms. Mac read out as I crossed, looking thrilled. "Whoa, girl! That was great!" She started reading the next times, and I walked up to Bean, who was cooling down just ahead.

"Well that was a lot of fun," he smiled. "Pop-Tarts for the Walkers. Nice job, Sis." We high-fived.

"You, too. What was your time?"

"6:10."

"Nice! But hey, next time? Shut up about the carrots."

Bean smiled. He was always trying to make some secret point that no one but him understood.

After class, Ms. Mac called Bean and I over and gave us our Pop-Tarts.

"I could trade this in for a bag of carrots, if you'd prefer Jeffery," Ms. Mac teased, holding his box away from his grasp. She knew the answer before Bean snagged the box from her hand.

"I'm looking forward to both of you on the track team this spring. Pretty sure I just found Graceford's milers. We start practice in March."

We nodded. Just like that, I was in love. I had found my sport.

It took me a while to get to sleep. When I woke the next day, Harey sitting up and ready for Friday, two thoughts were brimming, ready for my attention. My team, the Chicago Cubs, were World Series Champions. Bean and I were the champs of the Pop-Tart Mile.

Life was good.

A Walker Extra: One-Liner

Mine:

Uncle Toad, wielding a flashlight, before heading to the bathhouse one evening while camping, "Would anyone like to be accompanied to the bathhouse by a 'manly man?'"

Me: "And who would be the 'manly man?'"

Bean's:

Mr. Verbrecht said, "I don't remember taking the Illinois Constitution when I was in school."

Bean, "Had it been written yet?"

Mama's:

Mama said in a sweet voice before she left for work one Friday morning in November, "I'll have a real nice surprise for you when I get home."

Chapter Five

Wedding Bells

Wedding Whys:

1. Why does the preacher say, "You may kiss the bride." Why never, "You may kiss the groom." Why does the groom have to be the kiss starter?

2. Why does only the bride wear white? I know what that means, and think that both, or neither, should wear white.

3. If I go to a church wedding, does that count as my worship service for the week?

4. Have you ever been to a real wedding where, when the preacher says, "Does anyone here have a reason that this union should not take place? If so, speak now or forever hold your peace," and someone actually said, "Me! This is really a terrible idea!" Because, believe me, I'm giving it some serious thought.

5. If marriage really is forever, why is divorce a thing?

The Methodist Church of Graceford, on the east side of Main Street, was falling down. The ancient, stately building leaned, its foundation crumbling, which is ironic for a church if you think about it.

The replacement church is going up about two blocks from my front door. My travel time will be cut in half.

From the first week that we arrived in Graceford, I attended church with my Grandma Baker. Truth be told, I just wanted to recreate what I had known as Christmas Eve with my Grandma from our visits. It became quickly clear that a typical service couldn't be like the light and spiritual Christmas Eve service. But I kept going back. Attending church started becoming important to me for other, non-Christmas Eve reasons.

Family rumor has it that Grandma had a small stroke when my Aunt Nettie, Mama's younger sister, married a Catholic boy.

She wasn't upset that his name was Toad O'Brien. The fifth of nine children, Toad was of Catholic descent. Uncle Toad has a real first name, but Toad is all I've ever known. My Uncle Toad is one of the kindest, most gentle people you would ever want to meet. I've rarely seen him angry.

They attend something called mass. But when my grandma says it, and she says it often, she sneakily calls it mess. "Nettie, did you and your sweet husband," here she would give a squinty smile at my Uncle Toad, "take my darling Addy to mess this morning?" she would ask at Sunday dinner. If she ever had to say the word 'Catholic,' she would spit it out of her mouth like it was poison. She can be sneaky mean.

It makes me uncomfortable sometimes. Despite myself, I also think it is pretty funny.

I suppose Grandma would never be caught dead in a Catholic church, which seemed rather odd to me. Her buddy, God, was there, too, I thought. But she never missed a Sunday at the Graceford Methodist church. I liked it, too.

I started sneaking off to join Grandma Baker on Sunday mornings. Mama said it makes the rest of the family look bad when I am the only one there.

"Well, go with me, then," I would reply. But I knew they wouldn't.

Mama said she got tired of Grandma Baker sticking her nose right where it doesn't belong. That is, she would ask a lot of questions. Right there in front of God. And I guess Mama didn't want either God or Grandma to know what was going on at the Walnut Street Farmhouse on Saturday nights. Neither would have been pleased.

As it was, I would head out to the nine a.m. service and attach myself to Grandma's side. Grandma Baker sings like an angel. I try to match her vibrato. When I do, and he's around, Bean says it sounds like I am a wounded turkey. He's tone deaf. What does he know? For church, I don't usually wake him up. Madari has started coming too, which is another bonus.

Pastor Jim sometimes, in his sermons, talks about how he used to drink too much and called himself an alcoholic in front of the whole congregation. I think it's brave. But I also think that some people might stop coming to church if they know that their pastor drinks too much. Or used to, anyway.

Then, in what seemed like a sudden and premature move, Mama and Jerry announced wedding plans.

Grandma Baker switched directions about this real quick; first not wanting them to be together at all, and suddenly, insisting that they marry. Maybe she got tired of defending her daughter's decision to live in sin, especially to her Bible study group. But her victory? She convinced Mama and Jerry to be married in this new church. It was little consolation, but she would take what she could get.

As far as convincing these two lovebirds to get married, I'm pretty sure it was easy. Ever arm wrestled a three-year-old?

They decided on Christmas Eve. The first ones to be wed in the building, surely that would be something to proud of. And Grandma was excited to actually witness being in attendance at her oldest daughter's wedding, as opposed to Mama's first wedding, the one she only heard of from Nettie.

"Do you want them to get married?" I asked Grandma one day after school. We were finishing up the Advent calendar. It was done enough to be hanging up mid-December. We had about four ornaments to finish. We would finish today.

"Heidi, your mother is going to marry Jerry one way or another. I'm just trying to save her reputation."

"And yours?" I asked. Grandma made steady eye contact with me. I felt the tension.

"What's a reputation?" Addy asked.

"Something that I hope you never have to worry about, Addy," Grandma said sweetly. And then, to me, she answered my question. "It's not my reputation I'm concerned about. It's yours. And Jeffery's. People can be mean."

I knew what she meant. "Grandma, they already talk about us. I don't care. I really don't."

"I know! They do talk about you and Jeffery! They say you are fast!" Addy added brightly.

"What?" Grandma and I asked in chorus.

"Winners of the Pop-Tart mile!"

We laughed.

As we counted down the last few days of school before Christmas break, I wondered how this was all going to work out. It would be a busy time for sure. Mama, Bean, Uncle Billy, and I all had birthdays between December 22 and January 2. Then there was Christmas Eve, Christmas Day, New Years.

So, throw in a wedding? Christmas Eve? Sure! We've got time! You see what kind of grownups were running the show here, right?

On the last day before Christmas break, Mr. Verbrecht handed out our second quarter report cards. Graceford was one of the only school districts probably in the world that were still hand writing report cards. Which was fine with me. When we were in Evanston, our grades were all on a computer program which parents could check at any time. Fortunately, in my case, at Graceford Grade School, my grades remained to Mama what they should be. A complete mystery.

Until report card day.

Walking home, I needed to find a way to get Bean to forget about stupid report cards. I schemed to distract him. "What do you think you're getting for your birthday?" I tried to sound interested while stockpiling other topics to bring up. I needed to make his head spin.

"I already know I'm getting a running outfit. Hey, I'm going to give Mom a call to let her know about our report cards. She might be mad about that A- I got in social studies."

Seriously? "No, let's tell her when she gets home," I tried to sound sensible and calm. "We don't want to bother her at work. Her clients will get edgy."

"We won't bother her. We don't call that much—only if it is important."

"Report cards? You think that's important? Come on, Bean. I don't understand why we don't just let her know when she gets home."

"Because I want to let her know now! And I can." And here, Bean sprinted away. I immediately sprinted after him. More than once, I caught him, leapt with all my might, landed on his back and took him down. What was my plan? Holding him there forever? He was naturally faster than me, but adrenaline was on my side here.

We'd skirmish, and he would sprint out, only to gain a few dozen yards just to be tackled again. The way it turned out, once at our lovely little-reconditioned farmhouse, Bean got inside the door first and held it closed. This plan worked just fine for me, because as long as he was holding the door, he couldn't reach the home phone first. He tried to stretch around the corner to the kitchen while holding the door, but his arms simply couldn't reach the phone in its cradle.

Utilizing his only real move, Bean quickly locked the door, dashed to the kitchen, and punched in the number to Mama's work.

In a quick countermove, I unlocked the door with my key and fled inside.

"I should have asked for a smartphone for my birthday," Bean said under his breath. I knew it would take a while to get this call through to Mama. I still had time.

"May I speak to Joy Walker, please?" he panted into the phone, a giant dose of panic in his voice.

Adrenaline was flowing. We were both determined to win this battle. I had to make a strong move. I grabbed the biggest kitchen knife I could find, shocking both Bean and myself with this move.

"Put (bam). Down (bam) the phone (bam)." I demanded, slicing the vinyl piping around the top of the kitchen chair.

Bean was hopping side to side like a boxer on the far side of the table in the corner of the room. He was a little afraid, but he wasn't willing to put down the phone. So, I wasn't willing to put down the knife. I had him trapped.

"Nothing, why?" Bean said into the phone in a most unusual voice. "Oh, I just wanted to let you know we got our report cards today."

"Hang up!" I quietly demanded. Slice. Slice. The chair was taking a beating.

"Nothing's going on. Oh, that noise? Heidi. She's got a knife. She's trying to kill me. I got all A's on my report card. A- in history. Bye!" He hit the end button.

I slumped down on the newly designed chair and laid the knife on the table. I lost. The phone rang again, but we ignored it.

We celebrated Bean's fourteenth birthday the next day. First, he opened his gift; an all-blue, all-weather running outfit. I not only loved this running outfit he got for his birthday, but I wanted it. Then, we were heading out to get a real Christmas tree. I was pretty excited about this because Mama always asked Daddy if we could cut down our own tree. He always said no; always had his reasons not to. But the truth was, he one, didn't want to be around people he didn't know, and two, didn't want to take the time.

Jerry? The Cowboy-Hippy? "Happy to do it. By God, I know just the place to go."

Of course, he did.

So, on this freezing cold Thursday night in deep December, we crammed into his gray rustbucket and headed to who knows where. Everything seemed like a long drive from Graceford. In the dark, we set out to find the perfect tree.

The finding of the tree seemed perfectly easy, though we nearly froze. We all agreed on a big old spruce. It just looked friendly. The owner and Jerry cut it down, while we were sent inside with Mama. A kind but jittery woman made us hot cocoa with marshmallows. By my last, sweetest gulp, Jerry came in to announce that we were ready to go. The whole process only took about thirty minutes.

The only problem was, when we got home, we had about as many trees in the truck as we did when we left earlier that evening. That is to say, none.

"Son of a—*Oouch!*" Jerry yelled, kicking the back tire. It was rare to see him angry. But his composure returned quickly, Jerry declaring that our adventure, apparently, was not over. We clambered back in Rusty in search of our tree.

We found it, too, about a mile from the farm where we cut it down.

This time, Jerry tied it down with some frayed rope. It was only a little worse for the wear. One side lost some branches where it probably skidded along when it flew out of the truck. But how many people, really, could say that their Christmas tree, at one time, flew?

We set the tree up in front of the big picture window when we got home and decorated until the last minutes of Bean's birthday, complete with colored lights—no bubble lights, of course—loads of old-fashioned tinsel, strings of popcorn, and our favorite ornaments. My favorite, every year, was the red-eared beagle that looked like he was flying.

This year, near the top of the tree, we had a new ornament. A silver wreath, it said "Roadhouse, 12/24/16. Just Married." Mama and Jerry put it up together and then kissed right in front of us, making a disgusting sound.

I puckered my face and saw Bean out of the corner of my eye, squinting one eye nearly closed. Fortunately, Newt was asleep on the couch and missed this last public—Bean and I are people, after all—display of affection.

In the early morning of the eve of Christmas Eve, I was trying to convince myself that, minus the gross and flagrant smooch, we were going to be alright.

On Christmas Eve, my Mama, Joy Walker, became Joy Roadhouse. And Bean and I got a new stepdad and stepbrother.

It's a wonder we made it through this 'event.' Especially Grandma Baker.

Grandma's poor heart. It had rained or snowed most of the days of November, so construction on the church was put on a major hold, and it was becoming clear that it was 'highly unlikely' that it would be much more than a wooden structure by the Christmas Eve wedding.

Imagine her heart when she found out, if she ever did, that Jerry and Toad had drunk a few too many Budweiser's when they went to Kohl's to get black suits and ended up with lime green sports coats instead. Here might be a good time to mention Jerry's propensity toward cheapness. He was a real piker. I learned this word from Grandma. The green sports jackets were on clearance. Her poor eyes when she surely saw, and disapproved of, the suits. But she had no idea how many beers were imbibed in the dressing rooms of Kohl's itself. I feel sure that is for the best.

Imagine her heart when she heard that Saturday's forecast called for four inches of snow.

Finally, imagine her very soul when she heard that, after the rehearsal at the unfinished shelter, the ENTIRE wedding party, including her dear Reverend Jim, after many warnings, were escorted out of the Plain Good Restaurant for public disruption. No tickets or arrests were made, thank heavens. Even so, Grandma Baker surely didn't appreciate when Jerry, breath ripe with brew, put his arm around her, letting her know that he finally understood her fondness for her preacher.

"That Reverend Jim, he's one helluva guy, Dotty."

Still, despite the obstacles, the day came. Uncle Billy, Bean, and I took off early that Christmas Eve morning, to the nearby forest preserve. If it was summer, we would have gone for purple bee balms and happy looking Black-Eyed Susans. We were able to pull up a few salvageable cattails, which is easier said than done. They've got some deep roots, I do know that.

We cut some pine boughs and red berries and put them in mason jars. At home, I made ribbon out of burlap and tied bows around the jars. They looked pretty great.

I smoothed my off-white, lace dress, then pulled the braids out that I had put in the night before, perfectly waving my mousy brown hair, and even gave my bucked teeth an extra mid-morning brushing. And in an even more rare step, I brushed my cheeks with blush and put on a light dusting of eyeshadow and mascara. I knew the importance of this day to Mama, to Grandma Baker.

Coming downstairs, being careful not to step on my long skirt, Uncle Billy whistled, and said, "Mighty Heidi, you clean up real nice."

And so did he. Billy had also run something with teeth through his hair and had on an ironed white shirt and sharp looking grey pants. A shine gleamed off of his round glasses. Bean stood by Uncle Billy, his blonde hair combed to the side, wearing a light brown suit and a big smile that split his face in two. I felt proud to be his sister.

If you would have been a stranger to the two o'clock wedding scene, it is hard telling what would have stood out to you the most.

It may have been the way Jerry and Mama looked at each other, which almost made you want to turn your head.

It may have been the rafters and benches in this church which were really not much more than an idea. Honestly, the setting worked for Mama and Jerry, and my chest filled with pride seeing the way the green boughs and red berries brightened up the wooden sanctuary. Large snowflakes gently swirled and floated inside the church where the windows would eventually be as Bean and I walked Mama down the aisle.

It might have been the part in the vows where Bean, Newt, and I became real brothers and sister, sealed with our own rings to represent our joining. I feel like I'll always remember Newt with his serious face, punching his right hand into his left hand over and over like he wore a baseball glove, getting used to a ring on his finger for the first time.

It might have been the strange gathering of people. Llama farmers, employees of the grounds department, bikers and odd ducks. We were quite a diverse crew.

It may have been the chorus of chattering teeth. It was twenty-three degrees outside. And in. There was really no difference.

But the moment you couldn't forget was when Aunt Nettie, stepping back to grab the ring, slid on an icy spot before she fell face first onto the planked wooden floor. The solid sound stays with me yet. Uncle Toad jumped to his feet, grabbed the printed sermon from the hands of Reverend Jim, fanning Aunt Nettie for a long minute until she came to. Embarrassed about the attention, Aunt Nettie, face as red as a cherry tomato, insisted that she was fine. Uncle Toad stood right by her side.

When we left the rough and holy shelter that day, our lives were tied with Jerry, Newt, and even God forever. Boy, did I hope Mama knew what she was doing.

After the wedding, I started to realize that I may want things a certain way, like life to be simple with just Mama, Bean, and me, but that doesn't mean they will turn out how I want.

When I woke Christmas morning, I had a new family. I felt like I had a new Mama, too. I wasn't sure how I felt about that. I didn't want her to drift away again. I lay in bed and thought back to yesterday, to Mama and Jerry confessing their love for each other in that church just down the road. There was something about this that tore me in two. I had to admit that Mama and Jerry really did have a strong love for each other. A part of me, though, didn't want to see it. I felt like if I let myself see it, really shed my shell and feel this love, I would get sucked in. Only to be hurt later. I wasn't sure. I just wasn't sure. I suddenly remembered it was Christmas, and I was seriously souring my mood. I went downstairs, checking to see if Bean and Newt were still sleeping as I walked through Bean's room, and turned the lights on the tree when I got downstairs.

I grabbed my notebook.

1. We live in a cute home. Even Grandma Baker agrees. She told Mama, "It's got character, Joy."
2. It's Christmas!
3. No school until January 4.
4. My birthday is in four days. I'll be 13 years old!
5. Bean and I won the Pop-Tart Mile.

Usually, we all woke up early on Christmas morning, but I guess today was a honeymoon of sorts—the real honeymoon would take place in March, over Spring Break—so the newlyweds probably wanted to sleep in.

I thought back to Christmases when we lived in Evanston, when Bean and I would wake at five in the morning, feeling like we were going to explode waiting for our sleeping parents to arise. As much as Daddy was gone, I can't remember him being away on Christmas. He always came home for that. I wondered where he was right now. I wondered if he knew that Mama now had a different name.

And that she had started to drink.

As much as I told myself to relax about Mama's drinking, that it wasn't that big of a deal, I would counter-argue that I didn't understand why. Why would she even put one single toe down this crazy path? Mama was quick to tell Jeffery and me that we should stay away from alcohol. She said that this 'ism' that attaches itself to alcohol probably lived in her because her dad was an alcoholic. And there was a terrific chance that this beastly 'ism' lived in us, too, lurking from both sides.

And now, here she was, sitting by Jerry's side, drinking right alongside him.

Sometimes grown-ups make absolutely no sense at all.

Again, I reminded myself that it was Christmas, and pushed all that aside.

I needed a run.

I went back to the top of the stairs, trying not to wake my little brother. How strange was that? A little brother for Christmas. Actually, that was pretty cool.

"Beeanheead," I whispered, shaking his shoulder. "Get up!"

"Too early," was the muffled reply.

"Time for a Christmas run," I said, knowing that would do it.

Five minutes later, we closed the front door quietly behind us, not leaving a note because we knew it would be a while before these Roadhouses would wake.

As Bean and I ran through the streets of Graceford on this early Christmas morning, we reflected on the changes that the year had brought. Mama and Daddy getting a divorce, Mama getting remarried to Jerry, living in this small town.

"Do you think they are going to make it?"

Bean knew who I was talking about.

"They don't stand a chance." For the first time, I wondered what I wanted. I let in the idea that Mama deserved to be happy. Maybe Bean was wrong. Maybe it wasn't that they didn't stand a chance. Maybe none of us was giving them a chance. I knew I was growing pretty fond of young Newt. And being a big sister suited me.

Just last week, when Mama and Jerry told us three kids could choose between turkey and ham for Christmas dinner, we took Newt to the basement for a confidential meeting, and I explained, with Bean backing me up, that ham was not an option.

"Do you know what those black spots on ham are, Newt? It's poop."

Newt turned quickly and ran upstairs to make the group report.

We were eating turkey for Christmas.

As much as I liked Newt, though, the truth was, I didn't know what to make of this new union. But for today, I'd make the most of it.

I just didn't want to be stupid.

Especially since our double win in the Pop-Tart mile, Bean and I were running together at least a couple of times a week. Today, we ran about two and a half miles, and ended, like we often did, down at the fort. We had packed an army bag of goodies that we sometimes remembered to grab before we went. When we ran through our yard, Bean snagged it from the porch and took it with us. We hooked up our jimmy-rigged hammock chairs and swung for a while.

"Look over there, Heidi," Bean whispered. A thick, light orange cat was studying us from behind the far railroad track. When I stood to move toward the creature, he turned quickly and scampered away.

"Never seen him before. Have you?" I asked. After running and sweating, I was getting cold. I unhooked my chair and put it in the bag.

"Nope. I'll take the bag back. I'm going to go find that cat."

I got impatient, thinking of waiting to open presents until he got back. "Suit yourself, but don't be too long. It is Christmas."

I ran back home, and just as I expected, the house was quiet. I did a little extra banging in the kitchen, putting some cinnamon rolls in the oven, and the house came to life.

Before we knew it, our new Christmas tradition had begun. We opened presents, listened to carols, and started preparing the feast. We were hosting in our new home. Grandma Baker and Uncle Billy, Aunt Nettie and Uncle Toad, and little Addy were joining us today.

It hurt a little, knowing that less than a mile away, Grandma Baker's house stood empty, the one that held my most precious Christmas memories. But we had never hosted Christmas and having people at our home held some charm.

When Addy arrived, I was beyond excited. She rarely came to our house. We spent way more time at hers, and even more at Grandma Baker's. She hadn't seen our tree yet.

Though it was beautiful with its lights, ornaments, and long silver tinsel strands, try as we might, we just couldn't get the thing to stay upright in its old stand. It had fallen more than once, and was a little skimpy on one side, but that just gave it character.

"No worries," Jerry had said. "We'll tie it up with wire." And so, we did. Long wires, one end wrapped around the tree trunk, and the other to the locks on the window, secured our flying tree in place.

Bean was especially impressed with Jerry's handiwork.

Anyway, I invited Addy to come smell our beautiful and slightly crooked tree, bare on one side. I was quite insistent.

I then stepped up, point blank, to the tree and inhaled with all my might.

With my inhale, a single strand of tinsel entered my nostril and quickly traveled through my respiratory system, leaving only a small shiny tail sticking out the end of my nose.

Following Addy's instructions "DO NOT BREATHE," which I already knew because, when I did, I felt the trtrrtrtrtrttrtrtrtrt of the tinsel IN MY LUNG with the slightest movement of air, I held my breath. In fact, everyone in the room stopped breathing.

I slowly, slowly, slowly pulled the strand out. I held the culprit in between us in wonder and awe.

Sniffing tinsel clear down into your lung, or witnessing it for that matter, is one of those things that the mind just returns to regularly. I can still feel the vibration deep in my right lung when I think of it.

We spent the rest of that Christmas day, in our little renovated, relocated farmhouse, laughing and eating. Our misbehaving oven behaved pretty well, only throwing a fit when the rolls were warming up. They were unsalvageable.

Bean snuck a few, though. We sang while Uncle Billy played his guitar.

I fielded a hundred jokes about sniffing tinsel.

"Heidi, you could write a book about all the stupid things you do," Bean joked. Only, the funny part was, if I ever wrote a book—which I would never do because that is simply way too much work—it wouldn't be about the stupid things that I did. It would be about Bean.

I am sure that at some point, with many of the grownups, the drinking began. Jerry, Uncle Toad, Mama, even Uncle Billy was hiding a beer.

"Now be reasonable, Heidi. Not everybody who drinks is going to become an alcoholic. You're only scaring yourself because you have seen so many who have. But they don't all," I reassured myself.

It was Christmas. I took what I could get. It wasn't so much that I didn't have hard things going on in my life. It was just that, for some reason, at that moment, I could absorb them. I'd opened my protective shell. And when I lay my head down, my sweet cousin Addy with the ever-tight braids sleeping on the other side of Harey in my new room, I was filled with gratitude.

A Walker Trio Extra: Socks

Me: When I was little, my socks had to match my dress. Yes, dresses. It is all I would wear. I would throw a genuine fit if my socks didn't match. And I wanted my socks to be long–knee high. It caused me a lot of pain. Then one day, maybe because I was tired of being so upset about non-matching socks, I absolutely quit caring about them. Until I needed them. Then I just stole from Bean's sock drawer.

Bean: Bean is a sock genius. How he always is able to keep his sock drawer neat and full is truly a mystery to me. He must secretly wash, and maybe even bleach, his socks because he always has a beautiful selection. I would know.

Mama: Mama likes really thick socks all of the time. In the winter, her socks only fit in boots that would normally be way too big for her feet. Cabin socks, she calls them. I tried to steal Mama's socks, but I just can't stand them. In the summer, she doesn't wear socks at all. She's either barefooted or wearing her Birks.

Interlude One: Grandpa's Testimony

In the late fall of 1990, a 48-year-old man finished telling his story as the keynote speaker at a large and well attended Alcoholics Anonymous convention in Indianapolis, Indiana. His story was one of success, then loss, then tremendous growth in the restaurant/entertainment industry in the Midwest.

This tall and handsome former Air Force fighter pilot shared his tale of a face-first fall into addiction where he lost everything that was important to him, including his wife and two beautiful daughters. He explained how, after eighteen long, death-defying months on the streets, he started attending AA meetings. Slowly but surely, he rebuilt his life.

He spoke of 'letting go' of his past, making amends to himself, leaning on his sponsor, remarriage, and his dependence on the principles of A.A. His words were inspiring to everyone. Except for him. He could tell his story. But he just didn't feel it anymore. He was a terrific speaker, and he soaked up the praise of those who attended his session, but after the immediate satisfaction, he was empty. Surrounded by a crowd that wanted what he had, this man decided he didn't really want it anymore. He drove himself and his fifteen plus years of sobriety to a liquor store and found what he thought he might be looking for in an $8.90 bottle.

When this man woke up, maybe the next day, maybe three days later, in a county jail in Augusta, Georgia, he had absolutely no idea why he was there. Adding to his confusion, the guards regarded him like garbage and refused to respond when he asked where the hell he was, and why he was locked up. The man was stiff and a little scratched up. He found random cuts and scrapes all over his body. With no mirror to consult, he could only feel the painful cut and dried blood under his right eye.

After lunch alone, he was led into a meeting room where he met with a public defender.

"You going to tell me why I'm here? Nobody here will tell me," the man asked, panic streaking through his words.

"You really don't know?" the public defender eyed him suspiciously. The counselor could tell by the guy's face that he was telling the truth. He was lied to on a daily basis, however, so he wasn't sure. How could this man wreck so many lives and be so unaware?

"You want to know what you did? First, I'll tell you what you're charged with. Four counts of reckless homicide. Bring back anything at all?"

The man took in one sharp breath and held it there. "Reckless homicide? Did you say reckless homicide?"

"You drove your damn car into the back of a car full of teenagers; pushed them right in front of a train. All four of them died. That's what you did."

Chapter Six

Laundromat Birthday

What I love about my Birthday:

1. I catch up to Bean. Almost!
2. Sometimes it snows!!! Probably not today, though.
3. New running shoes! I hope, I hope, I hope!!!
4. Cheeseburger and fries today. OMG, I can't wait!
5. NO SCHOOL! It's still winter break for another week.

In the early morning of my thirteenth birthday, I had a dream of my Grandpa Baker. I didn't know what he looked like other than Mama's description, because once he left, she only saw pictures of his shoes. Grandma Baker had cut the rest of him out of their pictures.

When they were young, Mama and Aunt Nettie searched for their father, starting with looking for black shoes, wondering if the wearer of such shoes might be him. It made me glad that I knew what my handsome dad looked like.

In my dream, I sat cross-legged on our small front porch, wearing my favorite summer shorts. It was a dream. I wasn't the least bit cold. Snow fell steadily, when a tall stranger approached from a distance through the snow. The stranger wore a gray outfit and had chains on his hands. I knew that he had escaped from prison.

"Heidi. Where is my grandson? Where is Jeffery?"

"I don't have a brother," I lied to this stranger. He called Jeffery his grandson. "Who are you?"

"I am your grandfather. I need your brother. He is the only one who has the keys for these," he held up his arms with the chains. "I need to go free! I need to go free!"

I woke suddenly, warning bells ringing through my head before I realized what day it was. I forgot the dream quickly, my focus catching on the date.

It was December 29; my birthday. Today I turn thirteen!

My end of the year birthday is a reminder that good things can happen, even toward the very end of something.

But the very greatest part of my birthday is that the week of Bean being two whole years older than me was finally over. He was only one year ahead. As it should be.

The week before, though? Torture. Jokes like Jeffery's too old for the kid's table, but you're not. I wondered if this pain would ever end, if someday the tide might turn. I felt like it might, but I just couldn't really figure out how.

Last Thursday, Bean turned fourteen. For seven endless days, 168 miserable hours, 10,080 long minutes. I was only twelve. He never let me forget it.

Plans for my big day included the following: go to the laundromat in the morning, and then out to eat in the afternoon! Going out to eat was really a rarity for us, so I was super excited. First of all, when you live in the middle of nowhere, there are no restaurants. Second of all, with Mama and Jerry working in the town where all of the fun happened, they never wanted to make the half-hour trip once they made it back to Graceford.

I could already taste the cheeseburger, crinkly fries, and chocolate shake with real whipped cream that I would later enjoy.

Mama and Jerry dropped me off at about ten-fifteen. I insisted on getting the laundry done at the laundromat by myself. I think this is how I was thinking about it—if I kept busy the whole time, time would go faster. I washed and dried, smoothed and folded.

That morning, we had four baskets of clothes. There was only one other customer in the laundromat that day. Nosy Norma, who had only one basket. She was in and out pretty quickly.

I finished the laundry, I took it outside to the sidewalk, and then waited.

And waited.

The plan was that I would be picked up at noon. One o'clock came and went. Then two o'clock. It was pretty warm for a December day, about forty degrees with no wind, so I sat on the edge of the sidewalk outside Graceford Laundry. My excitement rolled to anger and then grew into dread. I was torn in two. Part of me couldn't imagine that I'd been forgotten. The other part wondered how I could have ever believed them in the first place.

At 1:25 p.m. Mrs. V. walked by the laundromat, talking to her doll.

At 2:33 p.m. A rusty red Ford Ranger showed up. Uncle Billy rolled down the window. "Growing roots out your butt, Mighty Heidi? You've been out here for over an hour. Need a lift?"

I shrugged my shoulders. It was all I could manage without tears. Once I opened my mouth, I knew they would roll. I was sick of those unwelcome things.

"What time were they supposed to come?" he asked, squinting his eyes. A question he did not really want to know the answer to.

I shook my head. I wasn't about to tell him.

Uncle Billy narrowed his eyes even more and bit his lip. He sucked in some major air, muttered some scrambled curse words, and then said, "Tell you what. Let me take you home. We'll see what's going on with your Grandma."

I shook my head. My toes were freezing, and my fingers numb. But I wasn't going anywhere.

"Wait in my car? It's nice and toasty."

Another head shake. I patted the empty spot on the sidewalk next to me. He parked, then quietly mumbling under his breath, sat down next to me.

After about ten minutes, Billy broke the silence. "Want me to beat 'em up for you?" I'm not sure if he was kidding or not.

I managed a tiny nod. In my misery, I cracked the slightest bit of a smile. I wasn't sure if I was kidding or not.

At three o'clock, Uncle Billy made a decision. He went inside, put a buck in the vending machine, pushed D8, grabbed a chocolate bar and came back out. He shoved the bar in my pocket with the fabric softener and with a smile that couldn't quite reach his eyes, said, "Sorry. I wish I could get you more for your birthday than this, well this little candy bar. It's all I got, baby girl. Happy Birthday, anyway."

On the short drive home, Billy told me if he were rich, he would build a five-story castle. He said I could be the queen of the whole operation. I would have new clothes every day and would never need to clean the dishes or do the laundry. There would be gardens in every color, a garden for food, and live music at every meal. I let myself imagine this for just a moment. Then I erected a wall that blocked both my ears and my brain from his words.

I appreciated what he was doing, I really did, but I was tired of dreams that rotted from the inside out.

Uncle Billy helped me carry the laundry in, then left. Bean was home. He knew that my birthday plans had been busted. He offered to play some games with me, but I wasn't up to it. I thought briefly of going over to Grandma Baker's house, or to Aunt Nettie and Uncle Toad's, but I couldn't bear the questions about Mama and Jerry. Especially Mama.

I went to my room, turned on the radio, and sat against my pillow and held Harey tightly while the tears flowed. I put the candy bar in my nightstand drawer, saving it for a happier time. The ground was slipping away under my feet. I wasn't really sure if I could trust anyone anymore.

The rest of that day and night, I imagined cops would show up at our front door with bad news. Would they come to tell us that Mama and Jerry were killed in some fiery crash?

Just last June, while we still lived in Evanston, I was at my friend Emma's, playing outside in our apartment courtyard one Saturday afternoon, when her mom came out crying. Her eyes were huge. She took Emma's shoulders in her hands.

"Emma, your dad has been in an accident on his motorcycle. He's ... He's ..."

She couldn't say it, and Emma just shook her head.

That whole day seemed so completely unreal. As police officers and strangers were in and out of their apartment, I couldn't wrap my head around how this could be happening. Hadn't he just cooked hamburgers on the grill for us a few days before? How could he be gone? How could Emma, whose dad was as alive as anyone else's the day before, have a dad who was dead today?

Now, I wondered if something similarly terrible had happened to Mom and Jerry. The possibility seemed very real. The alternative that they just got drunk and forgot seemed just as painful in a whole different way.

The slamming front door woke me from my sleep at 12:35 a.m., technically the day after my birthday. A hard knot of anger bloomed red and hot inside my chest. Mom and Jerry's voices traveled upstairs. They were arguing about someone flirting with someone else. I put my pillow over my head. At that moment, I decided not to care. I imagined myself surrounded by a hard shell: keeping me away from the world and keeping the world away from me. I would protect myself from hurt.

From them.

It was easier that way.

The next day, I stayed in my room. About noon Mama knocked on my door.

Here's what I wanted to say, "I am so angry with you right now that I don't even want to see your face. How could you? How could you have just forgotten about me on my BIRTHDAY! Leave me alone. And open your eyes. You have a problem!"

Here's what I did say. Absolutely nothing.

Because even though I was hurting, I just couldn't bring myself to let Mama know that I was angry with her. I just couldn't. But this one, I couldn't just absorb, either. Silence was my response. Still. I wasn't going to be nice.

She muttered something, but I couldn't really make it out. And I didn't care.

Bean was in and out of my room. At one point, he brought me some chicken noodle soup. At another, he brought me a fresh pair of socks. "No charge," he whispered.

That spoke volumes.

At some point in the day, I heard arguing downstairs, mostly Billy's voice, but once I heard Jerry say, "Don't you talk to my wife that way," to which Billy responded, "Fine. Don't treat my niece that way, and I'll shut up."

Then the voices quieted down.

"Heidi," I heard, paired with soft knocking. "Can I come in?"

I stood and opened the door. Uncle Billy came in, and Bean followed, carrying a rectangular box wrapped in paper. All over, in Mama's neat writing, the words, 'Happy December Birthday' were carefully written.

"I know it's from them, and I know you're mad, but open it." Bean held the box out to me.

"I already know. It's shoes," I said.

I wanted to laugh and cry all at once, and I did. I set Harey down for the first time since last night, and I ripped open the running shoes and put them on my feet.

"You know this means I can probably beat you now," I blubbered, giggling as I wiped away the snot, and feeling a little like a lunatic.

"I'd like to see that," Bean answered.

"Dessert?" Uncle Billy pulled a chocolate bar out of his pocket.

I jumped up and opened my nightstand drawer. "I've still got mine."

The three of us sat and ate our chocolate bars, Bean and Billy split theirs. While Uncle Billy told us how, during his brief track career at Graceford Grade School, he managed to knock down four hurdlers when he tripped over his hurdle and rolled into them, one after another.

"Young Billy Baker invents a new sport, 'When track and human bowling combine,'" Bean said in a sports announcer voice, using what was left of his candy bar for a mic.

I don't remember my first words to Mama, or Jerry, after my birthday, but I know for a while, there weren't many. And I didn't want to hear their apologies. I wanted to see an apology. I wanted them to act like the grownups that I needed them to be. Or, I decided, I didn't want them at all.

A Walker Trio Extra: What We Can't Live Without

Me: Harey the Bunny.

Bean: His science kits.

Mama: I'd rather not say. I wish it was me.

Chapter Seven

Burnt Brownies A Backdoor Burglar and Bouncing Bands

Facts About Uncle Billy

1. His glasses are round and thick.
2. He laughs a LOT. But be careful. His mood can turn quickly.
3. He has a song running through his head all the time. Just ask him. It's always something different. Sometimes, he makes up his own songs. Uncle Billy is very talented.
4. He can be wild and crazy. I've heard stories. But I find it hard to believe, because he is so good to Bean and me.
5. Billy says he's not going to live a long time because of his diabetes. When I think of him not being here, never being a father, I can barely stand it.

One Friday afternoon about a week after the new year began, Bean and I were playing a serious game of furniture tag. If furniture tag were an Olympic sport, we would have been medal contenders. Anything was fair game except the ground.

I was scaling the railing going upstairs, and Bean was crouched on top of a bookshelf, ready to leap onto the couch.

Uncle Billy came in. He was not the least bit phased by our positioning.

Instead of looking at us, he was staring at the ceiling. "How long's the leak been there?" he asked, nodding toward the drip, drip, drip.

"Started the last big snowfall," I answered. "'Bout two weeks ago, I guess. It's okay. I empty the bucket every few days."

Uncle Billy muttered to himself, shrugged it off, and went to the kitchen. "Looks like it's the three of us tonight, you ding dongs. Whatcha got to eat?"

He started rifling through the cabinets and the fridge. Then Billy started to slam doors, muttering under his breath. Even though he was angry, we knew he was on our side here.

He stood there for a few seconds. Then he took a deep breath, turned around, and forced a smile.

"What is it, Sir Bean and Madame Heidi, that you would like to eat for dinner?" he asked, followed by a flourishing bow.

"We've got rice. I think?" Sir Bean said brightly.

"You, your highness, will not be eating ..." and here, he trilled his 'r' for effect, "rrrice for dinner."

We loaded up into Billy's red Ford Ranger and headed to Adamsboro, the closest town that had a grocery store.

We followed our determined uncle around the grocery store as he collected the essential ingredients for dinner and brownies.

Pretty great.

We headed back to Graceford, arriving quickly, already tasting the delicious treat. We started with hot dogs and mac 'n cheese, then assembled the brownie mixture and placed it in the oven.

Now our oven, in terms of being a useful appliance, and much like the adults in our lives, sometimes did what it said it would do, and other times it did not. On this day, for some reason, mid-bake, the broiler kicked on to Super High, and in about fifteen minutes our brownie ingredients had burned to a black crisp, inedible even to Bean and me, which is definitely saying something. It brought back memories of eating charcoal with Bean, who insisted that the very insides would taste like chicken. Those scorched brownies were piping hot, but no match for the fired-up Billy. His cursing reached a new level as he tossed the burnt brownie mess into the front yard and ordered us back to his Ranger.

In a quiet but steamy ride, we returned to the six-mile-away Adamsboro grocery store in mere minutes, and this time had to run to keep up with Billy as he sprinted through the aisles, cursing the oven, Mom, Jerry, and anything else that came to mind.

In the checkout lane, he had long strands of hair standing on end, his round, thick glasses were fogged, and his expression of madness was unmistakable. We sprinted back to the car, flew home, and repeated the brownie making scene with a madman at the helm. He then did some type of voodoo to the oven, crouched in front of it, constantly and silently, and thirty-three minutes later, removed the beautiful brownies like Betty Crocker herself. He then calmly cut the brownies, they were hotter than blazes, but Bean and I didn't mention it, and watched us with delight as we ate the whole pan.

We offered Billy a brownie, but he declined.

"Don't like brownies," he simply said.

Our new family limped along. If we had food, Bean and I didn't see much. If we had money, we didn't see that, either. A large gap was growing between Mom and Jerry, and Bean and me. We were splitting into two units. They were staying out later and later and noticing us less and less. The only one willing to confront the truth was Uncle Billy.

The night of the brownie incident, he stayed on the couch and waited for Jerry and Mama to arrive home. About two in the morning, loud voices traveled upstairs. The Bean snuck into my room and went to sleep on a blanket on the floor. I threw him my bunny. He grabbed him by his arm and turned toward the wall. Arguing rose through my floor; Uncle Billy's voice mostly.

The next weekend brought a few welcome changes to 110 South Walnut Street. Jerry and Uncle Billy patched up the hole in the roof while Mama and I took Buzz to load up on groceries in Adamsboro. Jerry declared the wicked old stove good as new after spending an hour fiddling with the ignitor.

In an abrupt change, Mama and Jerry were home all weekend, spending time with us. It was strange.

Mama was on the couch reading a magazine when I came downstairs that Sunday morning, ready to sneak off to church.

"Hope you enjoy the service this morning," Mama called as I walked out the door. "Tell Mother I said 'hello.'"

I looked back at the house numbers on the way to the street, making sure that I had come from the right place.

The following Monday, Bean and I fell into our old routine. In theory, we weren't supposed to have guests in the house when our parents weren't home, but we'd disobeyed this rule so many times, we honestly forgot about it.

So, Tommy and Madari came over after school, as they often did. The four of us were watching YouTube videos of animals giving birth on Tommy's phone when Buzz pulled up in the driveway.

"You have to go," Bean told them.

Madari took off out the back door immediately. Tommy, however, ran up the stairs to retrieve his backpack up in Bean's room. He was running down the hallway when the front door opened. We shooed him toward the back door.

Cupboards nearly brimming, Mama started dinner right away. *Hooray for Uncle Billy*, I silently cheered. Pot roast, potatoes, dinner rolls, corn, a feast was on its way. On a Monday night.

"So, what happened in school today?" Jerry asked like this was normal when we sat down at the table.

"We got a big lecture from Mr. Verbrecht about being Upstanding Citizens when he is gone for the next few days," Bean explained. Suddenly, we heard a loud noise.

Thump. Thump. Thump. Thump. Thump. Thump from the basement just as we were digging in. Jerry was the first to respond.

"Someone's in the house," he whispered intensely, sitting straight up in his chair, every cell at attention. We stared at each other, trying to identify this new sound. Shoving himself away from the table, Jerry ran toward the back door and also the basement stairs.

"Get out of here!" Jerry yelled at the escapee. "Joy! It's a burglar!"

I rounded the corner just in time to see our friend Tommy dive through the air and out the back door, which was about four feet off the ground. Just a fraction of a second later, Jerry dove after him, grabbing toward Tommy's Converse All-Stars. Thank the Lord that Tommy was a fast-little booger. He rolled, ran around the house, trucking like lightning down the road.

With a quick look at each other, Bean and I decided to let Mom and Jerry believe that Tommy was indeed a burglar rather than fess up to breaking the family rules.

The next day in school, Tommy, walking with a slight limp, was a little sour.

"Thanks for helping me out last night, pals," he complained, but we knew he understood. "You could have at least saved me some pot roast. I smelled it the whole time. It was torture." And he did come for leftover pot roast, after school. We were sure to kick him and Madari out by five o'clock just in case the Miracle on Walnut Street happened again.

It didn't.

At the end of that week, Mr. Verbrecht was off to his two-day conference on Dealing with Difficult Students, the one he pre-warned us about. For a whole week, he lectured us, daily, on how we needed to be Upstanding Citizens for our substitute teacher, the frail and cranky Ms. Fann, whose fingers were fixed in such interesting sharp angles that our class would do nearly anything to get her to point, just for sheer entertainment.

'Where' quickly became our favorite word.

On Thursday, Mr. Verbrecht's nearly endless words stayed strong and loud in our heads. "I want nothing but good reports. Or you'll be sorry."

We took our spelling test, learned a little about the Civil war, ate lunch, played pickleball with Ms. Mac, diagramed some sentences, and in general, kept ourselves together.

Upstanding citizens?

Check.

Friday wielded a good beginning as well. We found that Ms. Fann had a funny side that none of us would have guessed. She told us that when she was a teacher, she, and many of the teachers, really, had the students make ceramic ashtrays for their mothers for Mother's Day. We thought she was joking. The thought that the school, this very school, actually promoted smoking?

"In fact, boys and girls, you know what I did to motivate my students to do well on tests? If everyone got an A or a B on a big test, I'd eat a cigarette. I really would," she cackled a bit mischievously, which opened up the door to let a little mischief into the classroom. And mischief stayed.

We were starting a physics unit in science and were going to build pulleys and levers to investigate speed and movement. Ms. Fann demonstrated with the model, and then we headed off to lunch.

Tommy, our class clown, still showing a slight limp, snagged the bag of rubber bands from the science supplies. At the lunch table, he passed them out, and as planned during Language Arts, when Ms. Fann was turned to the board, they started to fly. About half of our twenty-two students were members of this fast-developing rubber band gang, while the rest of us held tight to Mr. Verbrecht's words in our heads.

Sailing here, sailing there, the rubber bands went all over. The giggling was kept to a minimum, for the most part. Ms. Fann's hearing wasn't good. Even so, I couldn't help thinking that we were playing with fire here. I threw my energy into figuring out how to correct the sentences that Ms. Fann wrote on the board.

This next part happened as if in slow motion. Jacob Bruns, who never did have good aim, his nickname was Air Ball—sat directly behind me. In an almost imperceptible whisper, I heard him.

"One, two, three." Out of the corner of my eye, I witnessed a single red rubber band, in flight, elongated and wobbly, sail past my head. It traveled down the aisle and was headed straight for the back of Simone's head. Simone, just a smidgen before the band caught her, leaned her head on her left hand, at the same time giving out a soft, painful little sigh, allowing for the flight of the rubber weapon to sail just wide right and continue on. The band headed straight for the board itself when Ms. Fann, our substitute, ended her sentence with a period, turned around quickly, moving ever so slightly to her left, and stopped the flight of the little rubber joke when it bounced off her forehead.

The shot hit the Fann.

And we were dead.

Mr. Verbrecht returned the next Monday, so furious that he didn't say any of our names or make eye-contact with us all morning. We went through our lessons with a teaching robot. We just wanted the punishment over with already. Seeing him looking like he hated his job and didn't care about us? Heartbreaking.

After lunch, Mr. Verbrecht, still angry, burst open the subject which hung heavy and silent in the air all morning. Finally.

"I am, as you are all quite aware, very disappointed in your behavior with Ms. Fann. She left me a note, and this." He held out the red rubber band. "I have spent some time thinking of a consequence. You're all lucky that corporal punishment has been banned in our great state."

I had no idea what he was talking about but nodded my head up and down with my classmates.

"Instead of paddling you all, you all deserve two weeks of standing up against the wall at recess. Unless, of course, you all want some more trouble coming your way." He sounded like he meant it.

Okay, not too bad. We deserve it, I thought. And then a most terrible development took place. You see, deserve is not a word you should use lightly around Bean. Deserve implies guilt. Guilt implies personal responsibility. And my brother, my precise, justice-seeking, logic-driven brother, did not personally shoot a single rubber band. And so, I sat, eyes closed tight, in dreadful anticipation of the fallout that would come.

Maybe it wouldn't happen, I thought. Maybe, just this one time, he would let injustice slide. Didn't he stay quiet while the rubber band gang made their move? Didn't he laugh with the rest of us when the old substitute's eyes went wide with complete disbelief as the red welt spread between her eyebrows? Didn't he see how mad Mr. Verbrecht was? And when I opened my eyes, I knew. *Of course, not.*

Bean raised his hand high in the air.

A quiet groan moved throughout the classroom.

"Jeffery, I suggest, unless you have a life-threatening emergency, put your hand down," Mr. Verbrecht boomed.

His hand remained unmoved.

Tommy leaned toward his friend. Whispered something about not a good time. I could only nod in agreement and horror as the imposing teacher made it to Bean's desk in two long strides and towered over my brother. I could almost swear the big man was shaking. "I suggest you put your hand down, Jeffery unless you want to dig yourself a deeper hole than the one you are already in."

"Mr. Verbrecht," he began, in a voice that suggested he was completely oblivious to the precarious place he had just put himself in. "I personally did not shoot a rubber band Friday, and there are other people who didn't either, and I think that makes me and them exempt from standing against the wall at recess. I'd like to request that deeper hole, please."

"You what?"

"I said, I'll take what's behind curtain number two." His voice was calm, even jocular, but I knew better. My brother felt challenged.

Mr. Verbrecht ran a hand over his face. "Jeffery," he said, all muffled and behind his teeth. "Please put your hand down and ..." Maybe he saw the kamikaze look in Bean's eye, maybe he decided enough insubordination had happened that week. Either way, Mr. Verbrecht, our teacher who made us all homemade doughnuts just to show us the science of oil and heat, who was always ready to talk to a kid who needed guidance, Wonderful Mr. Verbrecht, snapped.

"Okay, perfect. You want number two, Jeffery Walker?" Here he was banging on Bean's desk. "You got it. Starting tomorrow, no, starting right now, you get to clean the toilets. The boys'— no, the boys' and the girls' and the STAFF toilets."

"I get to see the staff bathroom? I thought kids weren't allowed in there. I have always—"

"YOU WOULD BE HIGHLY ADVISED TO SHUT THAT TOOTHY MOUTH OF YOURS BEFORE IT GETS YOU INTO MORE TROUBLE." He took a deep breath, and when he spoke again, his voice was softer. Deadly calm. "You will clean the toilets after school until … well? You know what? Until Spring Break, young man." The hush that had fallen over the room got, if possible, more hushed.

But, at long last, the argument was settled. For the rest of this and next week, most of us would stand against the wall. And Bean, well, he seemed strangely pleased with his toilet deal. And during recess, as the Graceford eighth-grade class stood in a miserable but deserving line, Bean walked back and forth behind us, bouncing a basketball. All alone, but free.

A Walker Trio Extra: From the Kitchen

Me: Foods I can make: It starts with macaroni and cheese and branches out from there. Because my favorite foods are noodles and cheese. On the noodle side, I can make goulash, tuna casserole, ramen, and spaghetti. On the cheese side, grilled cheese, nachos, homemade pizza, and cheesy potatoes. And I can fry chicken.

Bean: The thing about Bean is that he has absolutely no table manners. Especially when he's hungry. It's amazing what he tries to shove in his mouth. Bean often gets sent to the other room to eat at home. At school, he does a little better. The upside is that he will eat absolutely anything. Which is good for our sometimes-working oven.

Mama: Mama has the appetite of a bird. It's a shame. Her best dish, though, has to be meatloaf and baked potatoes. She doesn't make it often. But when she does, it is good! Especially when she tops it with bacon.

Chapter Eight

Keeping Track

My Favorite Few who I hope to see today:

1. The stubborn and speedy Bean. Of course.
2. Madari, For sure.
3. Family—including Grandma Baker, Uncle Billy, Aunt Nettie and Uncle Toad, and my cousin Addy. A maybe.
4. Mr. Verbrecht and Ms. Mac. Most likely.
5. Mrs. V. Fifty-fifty chance.

PS: notice who is not on my list.

On a Saturday in mid-February, Mama and Jerry were making preparations for a big bash at our house, complete with one of Jerry's famous bonfires. "Even if it snows," he said. And it could. It was cold the Saturday morning of the party, dark clouds hanging low.

Most of the guests that were coming were from Mama and Jerry's work, or people that they knew from their running around, so I didn't know most of them. Mama said there wouldn't be any kids other than us; Newt was with his mom this weekend. So, I could go to Grandma's if I wanted to.

But I didn't. I needed to see how Mama handled herself at this party. This was a test. I hoped beyond hope that she would be okay, that she would be like she used to, like with Daddy. She would be paying attention to how much he drank, telling him to slow down.

"You've had too much already," she would chide, removing the bottle from his hand.

I hoped, tonight, she would do that with Jerry.

But hoping wasn't enough. I had to see. I decided I would glue myself to her side, no matter what. In fact, I had prepared. I drank very little liquid so I wouldn't have to go to the bathroom. I wore layers, and left my warmest coat, hat, and mittens near the door, so I wouldn't have to spend precious time searching. She wasn't going to shake me.

I helped Mama make some snacks: pinwheels, yogurt covered pretzels, Chex mix. I intentionally turned a blind eye to the large amount of alcohol filling the kitchen. Bottles of vodka, tequila, and wine crowded the counters. Coolers of beer were on the front porch. I reminded myself that I didn't really care who got drunk.

As long as it wasn't Mama.

The guests started arriving around seven. It was a friendly group, and I was reassured that even though I didn't know most of these people, they knew a lot about me. They asked about school, and some even knew about the Pop-Tart mile. *Mama must be proud.*

The flames from the bonfire must have risen ten feet high, licking the sky. The guests were having a great time. Jerry downed beer after beer but seemed mostly unchanged.

But Mama. Like it or not, I got my answer. She started out laughing and talking to her coworkers. She smiled at the stories swirling around her. As the night wore on, and with every little glass she downed, she disappeared a little more. By midnight, she was staring into the top of the fire, quiet, lost, and alone, even with me right next to her. I'd seen enough.

When I left, her eyes never left the flames.

I ran to the fort. When I got there, I found Bean.

"Some party," he said, sitting on his tree trunk. He had a bowl of Chex mix on his lap. The orange cat rubbed against Bean's leg, scratching his back.

"Yeah. Some party. The police are there now," I reported.

Bean lifted his eyes. "Really? Are Mama and Jerry in trouble?"

"Don't think so," I said. "They pulled up chairs and Jerry got them their favorite beer."

"Figures," Bean said. "Mom drinking?"

I stared up at the sky. Bean followed, looking up at the stars as well. "Know what I like about these? You can always count on them being there."

I nodded again. I used to think my Mama was a star.

I thought back to our first time here at the fort, when we had just arrived in Graceford. I remember wondering where Bean and I were headed. Here, staring at the same sky, I didn't like what I found.

"Bean, what's going to happen to us?"

"We're gonna survive," Bean answered, his voice tinged with anger.

"Is that it? Just survive?"

"We'll be okay, Hide. We'll be okay."

The next morning, Bean and I cleaned up, before too many people got a look. Frankly, it was a little embarrassing. Our yard was a big mess. As per our usual practice, we drank the remains of whatever was left in the cans and bottles. We knew it wasn't sanitary. We knew it wasn't smart. But it's just what we did. Always had.

I thought back to the little apartment in Evanston, to Sunday mornings after Daddy's long Saturday nights. Bean and I would scamper back to the 'back room,' complete with pool table and a little bar, and drink the remains of the cans and bottles. The taste of sulfur returned to me. Strangely, those were my favorites, the cans that were eventually doubled as an ashtray. We didn't talk about it, or think about it much, we just did it. Then we threw the trash away.

And here we were, doing it again. Only there were many more cans and bottles, and tiny little glasses with the tiniest drops of bitter liquid.

Poison. Maybe it was inevitable in my family. Maybe we were destined to be addicted to alcohol.

The thought made me sick.

I decided to skip church today, too. I didn't want to face Grandma Baker today. She was sure to have loads of questions. And God? I didn't want to face God much, either. They both loved me, this I knew. I just needed my distance, feeling too fragile to face their joint disappointment.

We had plenty of leftover alcohol from the big bash. Usually, Mama and Jerry drank away from home, so we didn't have much around the house. But now that we did, I had a chance to keep track of how much went missing. I started making light pencil marks on the bottles and counting the beer cans stashed in the back of the fridge. Even though they came home late, the amounts went down little by little, every day.

Mama had her own coffee cup, shaped like a light blue giraffe. The handle was the neck. She had a cup every morning before work, something she started as soon as she got her new job last fall. One morning, while in detective mode, I actually should have been studying for my spelling test, I took a swig of the very remains of her coffee cup to discover the same bitter taste that I had found in the little glasses outside after the bonfire. Mama left for work at seven in the morning. She was starting early.

Packing my bag for the day, I remembered that the first track practice was this afternoon. I pulled out my new running shoes. After I swiped a clean pair of socks from Bean's drawer, I pulled them on and did my best to erase the coffee cup discovery from my brain.

I saw Mrs. V. on the way to school that morning; a balm for my pain.

The school day crawled ahead like a backward-moving slug, but finally, we reached the final bell.

"You wearing shorts or tights, pal?" Madari called from the stall next to mine. In Illinois, in March, it could be 30 degrees or 65 degrees. We never knew. Today's temperature was in the 50's.

"Tights," I said.

Graceford didn't have enough money for an actual track, so track practice took place in various areas around the schoolyard. A big group of us headed out toward a side road, just west of the school, where we had run the Pop-Tart mile.

"Today, I am checking to see what you might be running in meets. Time trials. We will run an approximate 100 meter, an approximate 400 meter, and an approximate 800 meter. Everyone will run every distance. I want you to try your very best at each," Ms. Mac explained.

I was nervous and ready. I put a lot of hope into this going well, since our talk after the Pop-Tart mile. Actually, my desire to do well was something that had turned into something much more. A need. A part of who I was becoming. When I pictured myself running, I connected with—discovered really—some kind of strength that radiated from my core. Now I was a little afraid that I had misunderstood all of that.

But I was right to hope. While I didn't come in first in the 100 meters, I did in both the 400 and 800. Coach, after practice, told me that in order to improve my times, I would have to put in extra work. A few long runs in the mornings as well as on the weekends. She said the same to Bean. I think she knew that we had already been doing just that.

We would continue. It was a lifeline.

I even talked Madari into running with us sometimes. She didn't love it, but she was getting better.

Hurdles, that was Madari's event. "Not yet," she said one day at our house after practice, rubbing her scabbed knees when Uncle Billy offered to help her.

"I've got time to help out, Madari. I hurdled through my freshman year of high school."

"Um, I heard about you knocking down a whole heat of hurdlers. I don't know, pal."

Billy laughed. "My reputation proceeds me. Let me know if you need help."

I looked at my uncle. "You could meet us after school one day."

Madari shrugged.

"Whose school?" Billy asked.

"C'mon. Your school, Smarty."

"I dropped out."

Bean's head snapped up from his homework. "What?"

"It's no big deal for me. It is for you guys. You're going to live long lives. I'm not. It really doesn't matter if I have a high school diploma or not."

I shook my head. "It does matter! You don't know the future. You can't just give up. Seriously? You would never let us do that."

Billy said this next part slowly, like he was holding himself together. "Everyone thinks they know me better than I do. I'm sick of it." He stood up and went to the door, looked back like he was going to say something else, then shook it off and walked out.

"Are you kidding me?" I said. The three of us looked at each other and shook our heads.

When we ran in the mornings, Mama was adding more vodka to her coffee. When we ran on the weekends, Mama and Jerry went off to their mysterious world. Jerry, who always had, almost no matter what, been cheerful and chipper, was becoming moody and angry.

When I found out that our first track meet was scheduled on the Tuesday of Spring Break, I was upset. "Can't I just stay with Grandma Baker?" I pleaded. "I don't want to go on your dumb honeymoon, anyway. And shouldn't you and Jerry be alone?"

Bean didn't seem as upset.

"We hardly ever get to do anything fun." Easy for him to say. Uncle Toad said he was going to take him out on a boat. I didn't want to go on a boat. I wanted to run my very first track meet.

But I was going to have to wait.

A Walker Trio Extra: Sleep

Me: I need it worse than anybody. Wake easy. When we used to stay out late, I would go up to Mama, pull on her shirt sleeve, and say, "Let's get me home and get me to sleep." I love sleepovers, but I don't stay up late. Ever.

Bean: Doesn't really need it. When we used to be out late, and we were little, Bean would be hiding somewhere Mama couldn't find him. Eventually, she learned that she could probably find him in a drawer.

Mama: Can take it or leave it, but when sleeping, sleeps heavy. A lot of experiments happened while Mama took naps, especially when we were little. When she sleeps, she likes it to be dark.

Chapter Nine

Spring Broken

What you might find if you see the Walker/ Roadhouse/O'Brien clan on vacation:

1. The kids will be searching for playground equipment for some serious playground tag.
2. All of the adults may be drunk, except for Aunt Nettie.
3. Cowboy-hippy Jerry Roadhouse is likely to talk your head clean off.
4. The party goes late!
5. Only a few of us are good singers around the campfire.

When the time came to leave for our trip, I was pretty excited. Mostly because the O'Brien clan was joining us. Addy and I stood outside of the truck and jumped around in circles, arms interlocked.

"We're going on vacation. We're going on vacation," we sang.

I got to ride in Uncle Toad and Aunt Nettie's car while Bean and Newt rode in the cramped backseat of Rusty.

Somewhere in West Central Indiana, we stopped at a sit-down diner for lunch. We kids were allowed to sit at our own booth, and the grownups were at a table close by. A pretty young waitress,

Leslie, took our orders, and did we feel like big shots ordering on our own. She smiled at us, and we smiled back, nice as you please.

"Seven-dollar limit," Jerry shouted over to our table.

"Okay," we easily agreed. Jeffery and I helped Newt and Addy in order to keep within our money limit. Addy ordered oatmeal, Newt got a bowl of chicken noodle soup. Bean and I ordered cheeseburgers and fries.

The noodle soup came first as Leslie set the big bowl smack in front of Newt, then turned to walk away.

Our eyes were all drawn to it at once. A fat and curly black hair floated on the top of the broth. Newt gave out a little yelp, which earned the attention of Leslie.

"Is there a problem?" asked Leslie, returning to us.

Now why this single hair was so funny to us, I'll never know. It just was. Like that hair was the best joke we had ever seen.

I sucked in my cheeks and dug my nails into my legs to keep from bursting out.

Then Bean said, "Uh ... does the hair cost extra? We've got a seven-dollar limit."

That was it. It was over, we were slain. The four of us burst. It was embarrassing. Newt started banging the table, maybe in a strange effort to get a solitary breath back into his lungs.

I looked over at the parent table, and the angry faces only made us laugh more. Oh, they were mad.

Our waitress, Leslie, our Leslie, was standing at the kitchen door, tears welling in her eyes, because of us.

Ninety-nine of one-hundred times, this would have sobered me up in an instant. But because of the strength of this wave of hilarity, it only seemed funnier in that moment.

We were a mess. Despite stern warnings from the parents, none of us could gain control. My sides and stomach screamed with pain.

Two of us—I won't say who—peed their shorts, just a little. Finally, Mama and Nettie shuffled us outside and threatened to beat us.

"That poor girl in there is crying," Mama said, who held Bean and me responsible because of our age. "Get yourselves together. Now!"

What I wanted to say was, "I'm really sorry." But another ill-timed, "Bwahaha," was my response instead.

"You stay right here on the sidewalk until you can stop being so incredibly rude, all of you," said Mama, and she and Nettie went inside.

We could not grasp control. We didn't deserve to eat. But have you ever had to vomit? No matter how much you want to hold it in, you can't. It's going to come out. That's how this laughing was. Finally, it slowed, coming in tired, painful bursts.

A few minutes later, Uncle Toad brought our meals, all to-go style, out to the sidewalk.

"I'm really disappointed in you kids," he said. Uncle Toad? Disappointed? That was it, the very end of our joint outburst. We ate in a tight circle. Hurting in our middles. Feeling like terrible people. Even when Newt opened his cup of soup, free of the culprit hair that started the whole thing, we just quietly ate.

We were going to hell. We all knew it.

The adults' anger and our guilt slowly dissolved on our quiet drive toward the center of Indiana. I had been reassigned to Rusty the truck due to our outburst. Addy and I understood.

This part of our trip was some kind of surprise. That night, we all got dolled up, most of us wearing the clothes we wore at the wedding a few months before, Aunt Nettie with her same crimson dress, and Mama, the only one with new clothes, wore a dress that was silky and light blue.

"They look like movie stars," Addy whispered to me, and I agreed. Mama and Nettie had an excited glow about them.

Finally, the secret was revealed.

"We are going to meet your Grandpa Baker," Mama told all of us.

Grandpa Baker? Hadn't Grandpa Baker been in jail? Wasn't he a drunk? Would he shoot Bean if he said something wrong, which he was sure to do? I wasn't sure about any of this.

Here was the plan. Mom and Nettie had been in touch with Grandpa's new wife. They owned a restaurant near Indianapolis.

I pictured a saloon and a dartboard.

We were going to go to that restaurant and surprise this post-prison Grandpa. So, Mama and Jerry, Nettie and Toad, Bean, Newt, and Addy and I would just go to a table and ask for the owner. He would come to the table and see his daughters— who he hadn't seen since they were four and seven—and their families? And then what? Go to the next table to make sure those customers had their steaks cooked to their liking and full drink glasses?

Oh, the possible ways this plan could go wrong.

I kept my eye on Bean, dressed in his light brown suit, as it could very likely be the last time I would see him. For some reason I imagined him getting shot by the end of the night by my own mother's father. I couldn't get the thought of my grandpa having been in prison out of my mind. It completely defined my image of him. I also couldn't help thinking of the dream that I had of Grandpa Baker on my birthday. That didn't ease my nervousness one bit.

When we walked into the restaurant, I was shocked. From the look on his face, I could tell that Bean was, too. First of all, the restaurant was the nicest I'd ever been to. Glass tabletops, white napkins, well-dressed staff. Grandpa's wife, Meg, met us at the door and led us to a round table where we were seated. Meg was a distinguished looking woman who reminded me a bit of my Grandma Baker in her elegance. Her dark hair was piled tightly and stylishly on her head, and she wore a dark blue suit. I liked Meg immediately.

After ordering our drinks, we waited anxiously as Meg let Grandpa know that the customers at Table 38 required his attention. My heart pounded.

A tall, handsome man with a peaceful, friendly face, long legs, and round blue eyes the color of the edge of the sky strolled across the room looking toward Table 38. He was the kind of person who looked like he had answers and would not hesitate to share them with you.

I have to say, part of the power of this moment had to do with the way that I had always looked at alcoholism. Two things happened at once. My hatred toward the disease itself grew, and the understanding that the disease and the person are not necessarily the same thing blossomed. What I could tell instantly was this, my grandpa was a great guy who battled a fierce beast.

As he approached, something on his face began to change. He slowed his pace and then stopped in his tracks. His eyes went wide with recognition. He clasped his mouth, and the tears immediately began to drop down his face.

Can you imagine seeing your adult daughters for the first time in decades? I imagine he recognized the way his daughters smiled, the angles at which they held their heads. And the color of their eyes, light blue, like the edge of the sky. Matched sets.

Grandpa Baker put his hands on his knees and swayed. Mama and Aunt Nettie stood up at Table 38 and went to him, holding him up as they all embraced. Everyone in the room could feel the mending of broken hearts.

It was at this rejoining of lives that I began to understand that you can really have the wrong idea about someone or their life, especially if you just get a little information about them. Grandpa Baker was one of the kindest, smartest people I had ever met.

Grandpa asked all of us, his grandchildren, lots of questions. About school, about how we liked to spend our time, about our dreams. He was so easy to talk to. So was Meg. We fit together like pieces of a puzzle.

At the same time, I thought of me, drinking whatever was left at the bottom of someone else's bottle, which I had done time and time again. I wondered about my own future, and what kind of a puzzle piece I was in the big picture. Part of me wanted to fit in. Part of me wanted to fit into another puzzle altogether. Regardless, It was an evening to remember.

From Indianapolis, we headed to South Haven, Michigan, where we would stay for the remainder of our vacation. Jerry led the way in good old Rusty, the camper behind, as we entered the state park. We found a couple of good sites and set up camp. What shocked me was the amount of beer that Jerry and Uncle Toad brought along. I counted five cases. That's sixty beers, basically between three grown-ups. I could not fathom how they could physically drink that much in a week. Then Jerry said something that shocked me even more; he and Toad, in the morning, were going to the closest town to get more alcohol. They didn't have enough. *How?*

So bright and early the next morning, Jerry and Uncle Toad headed to town, and we kids began exploring the area. We spotted a large, wooden play structure, and decided to stop.

"Looks pretty rickety," Newt observed.

Bean went up to it and gave it a solid kick.

"It's fine," he proclaimed. "Who's It?" he asked.

We couldn't pass up a perfectly good game of playground tag when it presented itself.

The rules were simple. No touching the ground. Only ten seconds at a time on base, which was a small chain-link bridge in the middle of the structure. I volunteered to be 'it.'

Away we went. Jumping, leaping, sliding, Newt, Addy, Bean and I were flying around the wooden structures.

I caught Newt quickly, and he caught Addy quickly. Then, in an unexpected development, young Addy caught Bean. And it wasn't because

Bean let Addy catch him. He was far too competitive for that, even though he adored his little cousin. Or that Addy was especially good at playground tag. To be perfectly fair, she had far too much parental supervision to be on the same expert level as Bean and me.

No. Addy caught him fair and square because just before he was tagged, he was sliding down an old round wooden pole. And as he was sliding down, his skin overlapped the tiny edge of an unattached, triangular shaped shard of wood.

The further Bean slid, the further the wooden wedge entered the tender skin just at his upper thigh.

Until he reached a point where he could slide no more.

"You're It," Addy said. It had been too easy. Bean didn't move.

In fact, Bean held on to the pole for dear life, held securely by the pain of a four to five-inch wooden splinter in his groin, bright red blood gathering around the brownish gray edge of the wood.

We stared for a moment, wondering what we were going to do. "Hide! I can't see it," Bean nearly complained.

"You don't want to," Newt breathed. He turned to me. "What do we do?"

I looked at Addy and Newt. "Do you guys know how to get back to the campsite?" Their puzzled faces revealed the answer. I was pretty sure I remembered the way. "You guys stay here. I'm getting help."

"Help? How bad is it?"

"Bad!" Newt and Addy sang in chorus.

"Naw. Heck, it's not that bad. Just hang tight." Did he really have a choice? "I'll be right back."

I ran through the wilderness, looking for areas where we had knocked over the tall grass. Up ahead, I saw the beginnings of the camping area. Relieved, I turned on the burners.

When I returned to the campsite alone, Mama and Aunt Nettie were certainly surprised. "What?" Mama cried.

"Where's Addy? And Jeffery and Newt?" Added Aunt Nettie while I caught my breath.

"Bean is stuck … On a pole … A big piece of wood … Do we have … A saw?"

"What? Slow down, Heidi. You aren't making sense."

I closed my eyes and took a couple of deep breaths. Then I took a stab at explaining. "We were playing playground tag on a wooden structure back that way. Bean was sliding down a wooden pole. A huge splinter entered his leg here," and I pointed to my inner thigh "and is poking into his leg all the way up to here," and I pointed to the upper inside of my leg. "He's stuck."

A campsite neighbor who overheard our conversation walked confidently over to us. "I'm

Mel, an EMT. I have a golf cart. And a tiny serrated knife if we need one."

"Well, apparently, since our idiot husbands have all but abandoned us out here, it looks like we do," Mama said. "Thank you!"

We hustled to the golf cart, hopping on as Mel zipped along, following my directions. We found Bean, still suspended in air, and Addy and Newt, just as I had left them. Only now, they both held Bean up on the undersides of his legs, beads of sweat bursting from their foreheads.

Mel, our new friend, took charge. She talked calmly to him while she ever so gingerly sawed away at the offending wood with the teensy tiny knife, "We'll have you off in a jiffy, son. So, your sister here calls you Bean. Must be a good story there."

Once free, Bean leaned backward into Mel while she lowered him to the ground, splinter still in the skin.

"I'll take care of that real easy-like when we get back to camp, Bean," she assured us all. There wasn't room for all of us on the golf cart. Addy and I walked back.

"Do you think he'll ever be able to have kids now?" Addy asked.

Now how did my little cousin come up with that question?

When we returned, Bean was lying down, limp but splinter-less, on a long lawn chair. Newt lay next to him in his own chair, keeping company. Mama and Nettie were upset, saying something about 'those idiots' bringing their families to a good for nothing campground, and waited for the men to get back.

Their wait was a long one. 'The idiots' didn't get back until after two in the morning, Toad being passed out in the driver's seat of Rusty. Then there was all kinds of shouting and shushing. You can't really have a private screaming conversation at a campground. The only quiet one was Toad. In his unmoving state, he didn't say a thing.

As the next day went along, the talking returned, except for Aunt Nettie, who silently fumed at everyone except for us kids. We spent our days on the sandy beach, running up and down the dunes, the lake water was much too cold to swim, on the playgrounds, we all agreed to no more playground tag this week and romping around the campground.

Of course, Jerry met some friends, and their families spent time with ours as we spent the sunny days and chilly nights and had what the grownups seemed to think was a great time.

The second to the last day, Uncle Toad got us tickets to ride a pirate ship boat, and we sailed around the edges of the lake and through a river. Lots of people fished along the edge of the boat. We cruised along, bobbing up and down. Bean looked like he was in heaven.

On the last full day of our trip, I noticed Mama going to the cooler an awful lot. I counted beers all afternoon. Once nighttime came, and we sat around the campfire, Mama was slurring her words and laughing too loud. It reminded me of Daddy. It reminded me of distance, someone being far, far away. I started to feel sick.

Mama was sitting on our long lawn chair. I started to walk toward the camper, ready to get away, when she called me over to her.

"C'mere, lil' monkey. Come shee your Mama monkey," she slurred, much too slowly patting the plastic arm of the chair. I thought of a trip to the zoo, long ago, when we sat for hours in the Monkey House and watched a mama monkey groom her baby. Hot tears formed in the corner of my eyes.

Part of me wanted to run to her and have her hug and hold me, and part of me wanted to run away so I wouldn't see the path she was headed down.

That night, I chose to go to her.

I sat between her legs and leaned into her as she held me close with one arm and fed her brand-new addiction with her other. I fell asleep, smelling her beer breath on the top of my head, with my heart breaking, knowing that we could not stay this way.

I was ready to go home.

The following Tuesday, I woke up ready to run my first track meet ever. I imagined everything about this moment from the time I crossed the finish line during the Pop-Tart mile. We were running at Adamsboro Township High School, the place where I would be starting high school in just four short months. When we pulled up to the school, buses lined the road. There were at least ten junior high schools competing today. My excitement turned to pure nerves.

I could feel my heartbeat in my neck.

Madari, who had competed in the meet that took place over Spring Break, was giving me tips. Warm up in your regular running shoes, wear lots of layers in case it gets cold, don't go out too fast. She was trying to help, but it made me crazy. I made an excuse to go to the bathroom so I could be alone.

I remembered how excited I was just to run. And I reminded myself that, though this was a great opportunity, I was going to have fun.

Forty-five minutes later I was in the staging area, ready for my first official mile. Ms. Mac, who was timing at the finish line, came up to me. "Don't think about it too much, Heidi. Just go out there and do what you do. Run your pace like we have practiced."

"All eighth-grade 1600 runners. Step on to the track." They lined us up, raised the gun, and bang, we were off.

Just like the Pop-Tart mile, I didn't start out in the lead. But I stayed with the lead group. And just like the Pop-Tart mile, I finished second. My time was six minutes and thirty-six seconds.

I watched Madari sail over the hurdles with a grace and a strength I didn't know she had.

I earned second place medal for my time in the 1600. I caught two people when I ran the 4X400 relay, and our team placed fifth.

As I walked to the bus after the meet, I was tired but dizzy with excitement. I loved running. It was official.

A Walker Trio Extra: Most Asked Question

Me: "Will it be okay?"

❀

Bean: "Does that make sense?"

❀

Mama: (To Me) "Can we just give it a try?"
(To Bean) "What were you thinking?"

Chapter Ten

Spiraling Downward

Why I Just Might Stop Writing Lists:

1. I need to start remembering on my own.
2. I'm tired of running out of notebooks.
3. I have too many lists.
4. I'm tired.
5. Because Bean doesn't mind my lists anymore.

Things in the relocated farmhouse were sketchy. The one-time small hole in the ceiling had returned in a large way, as an ugly open mouth. Food was scarce. Parents were scarce. As much as I hated to, I found it best to steer clear of both Grandma Baker and Aunt Nettie, who were asking too many questions.

They were good questions, actually. They just didn't have good answers.

Bean, who also loved track season, was otherwise grouchy.

He knocked on my door one evening after a long run and cereal for dinner. His face was stony. He had a list and was about ready to read me my most recent sock money invoice. I didn't want to hear it.

Evidently, my tab crossed the three-hundred-dollar mark. I took the invoice out of his hand, tore it to pieces, and stormed past him. And without asking, I took possession of his favorite running pants right out of his drawer. The blue all-weather running pants from Bean received for his birthday were mine now. A silent war had begun. Were Bean and I turning on each other?

Track meets were about the only things that were keeping me going. It was the reason I did some—not all—of my homework. It was the reason I wanted to get up in the morning.

The morning of Sectionals, the big meet of the year, the one where we could qualify for the Illinois State Championships, I pulled on my uniform and Bean's blue running pants and headed to the bus. Graceford was hosting the meet at Adamsboro High School.

Coach Mac had talked about this meet all season long. Only the top runner got an automatic bid to State. The only other way to qualify was to hit a qualifying time. My best 1600 time so far this season was a 6:12. I needed a 6:01 to qualify. "It's sure possible, but that's quite a bit of time to shave off," Mrs. Mac explained when I asked if I had a shot.

She wanted me to get a personal best; better than 6:12. She said qualifying for state would just be gravy.

Since we were hosting this meet, our parents were asked to volunteer to help run it. Some helped with field events, others held the exchange flags. Last week Coach Mac called Mama and Jerry to ask whether they could help with the concession stand. I was mortified. Fortunately, the concession stand was hidden away from the track. I wouldn't have to see them.

Uncle Billy came over to our tent before the race, sporting an ancient Graceford Track sweatshirt. *Where'd he come up with that?*

"Ready to run, Mighty Heidi?"

"Yeah, sure. Only wish they weren't here." I nodded in the direction of the concession stand.

"Block 'em out, Kiddo. That's what you runners do, isn't it? Block everything out?" I guess he was right. That's what I liked about it.

"Go get 'em, Heidi. You got this. And no matter what, I'm really, really proud of you."

I took his sideways hug then ran to the staging area.

Uncle Billy and Bean set up at the 200-meter mark. Mama and Jerry being at this meet really needled me. First of all, they hadn't been to any of my meets so far. I was okay with that, really. It was my own thing, protected from the wounds that our family displayed so obviously. Second, I could tell they had been drinking, just by the brief time we had seen each other before the events began.

"I can't wait to see you run, Hide," Mama said with a slight slur.

I shook my head. "You won't be able to see me, Mom. The concession stand faces away from the track. I'll come tell you how it went as soon as we are done. Promise."

Jerry just laughed. "Oh, we'll find a way to see you run."

I didn't like how he said it.

The gun blasted, and I took off.

"Strong and steady, Mighty Heidi," Uncle Billy yelled as I passed the 200 mark the first time, in third place.

"Keep your head up, Hide," shouted Bean.

When I got to the 300 mark, close to the concession stand, Mama and Jerry were hanging out the front, yelling like lunatics.

"That's my girl," Mama yelled, arms flailing wildly. "Run, Heidi! Faster! Catch that girl in first place!"

I ignored them and looked toward Coach Mac, who was ready with my first lap time.

"1:31, Heidi. Good. Let's keep that pace."

I headed around the curve, headed back to Bean and Uncle Billy, who were standing outside of the fence, Billy with a stopwatch.

They yelled, and I motored on. Strong and steady. Strong and steady.

This time, when I passed the stand, Mama was on Jerry's back, yelling something about, "my girl."

On my last lap, I turned on the burners and blocked everything out. I passed the runner in second place. If Mama and Jerry would have been standing on the track, I wouldn't have noticed.

When I entered the final stretch, my legs burned. I knew I was almost done. I wanted to hear 6:01.

As I came close to the finish line, only several more yards to go, I listened for times. 6:02 … 6:03 … 6:04 …

And I leaned across the line.

"6:05, Walker. Second place. Great job. You can step off the track," the official told me at the finish line. I didn't qualify for state. Four seconds. While I was starting to count in my head the difference between qualifying and not qualifying, *One, one-thousand, two, one-thousand,* I turned to see if it was safe to leave the track when I spotted Mama and Jerry, yelling and running down the track, handing out popcorn to the stunned runners, even the ones trying to finish the race. They were headed my way.

Oh, God, Oh, God, Oh God, my mind repeated. I sprinted off the track and to the tent, going right past my coach, who may or may not have been trying to talk to me. While picking up my things, I turned to see Jerry being restrained by a coach. Mama was pleading with them.

Uncle Billy and Bean met me by the tent.

"Get me out of here," I said to Uncle Billy. "They ruin everything." Billy nodded his head and walked over to Coach Mac.

Bean put his hand on my shoulder. "Great race, Heidi. You looked strong."

The race! I'd forgotten it already, thinking of Mama and Jerry. I was filled with a swirl of emotions. A seven-second personal best, but no state qualification. I was so close. Uncle Billy came back.

"Coach told me to tell you 'great, great race.' She is so proud of you. Also, she said why don't I take you out for a little while and come back in time for Bean's race. She doesn't think you'll want to miss that. They are being asked to leave, so you don't have to worry about them." He turned to Bean. "You be okay?"

Bean nodded. We knew he would be, at least on the outside.

We left to walk around the forest preserve, looking at the new buds on the plants and trees.

"I am back in school," Billy told me as we walked. "You were right. I'm not giving up. I would be furious with you if you did. And I figure you need a few good role models."

I nodded. "Good. You were born to do great things."

"You, too, Heidi. I really wanted to make State in the hurdles, and I was close, but I got sick. I can't wait to cheer you on when you get there."

I started to argue and stopped. I would go to State, sooner or later, I decided. I would do it for me, and I would do it for him.

We returned to the meet later. Bean placed in both the 1600 and 800. When Uncle Billy brought us back to Graceford, Mama sat at the kitchen table, holding tight to her giraffe cup.

"Jerry's in jail," she said, running her finger across the giraffe's neck. Like that was all that mattered.

"And both of your kids ran great in the Sectional track meet."

Maybe she didn't know what to say, how to bridge the gap that grew even further that day. Maybe she didn't care. But for whatever reason, she picked up her phone, stood up, and walked out of the room without saying another word, with so much left to be said.

While I opened up cans of soup to heat on the stove, Billy flipped the grilled cheese he was browning on the skillet. "Joy does care. I know that," he smooshed the bread to heat the cheese. "She's just lost right now."

I could tell he was trying to convince himself as much as convince us.

Bean was pulling plates from the cupboard. He still had his track uniform on. "We don't really need them."

I stepped over to smell Mama's cup, the bitter taste strong.

Bean was right. We didn't need them. We couldn't afford to. Problem was, we couldn't afford not to, either. Jerry was in jail, and we were in prison. If there was a key, I sure as heck didn't know what it looked like or where it was hidden.

Mama never did apologize for that day. And I didn't really expect it. Maybe there weren't words that were big enough to cover the hurt.

Jerry was only in jail overnight, charged with drunk and disorderly conduct. Murmurs of court dates and probation swirled. Actually, Mama and Jerry were around a little more often during the month of May, not staying out late after work like before. But Mama dropped to a new level of sad. Jerry's mood? Angry. They both were quiet. Unless they were fighting.

Uncle Billy's graduation from Adamsboro High School was a big deal. Bigger than most high school graduations. I wondered how many big moments he had left. I knew how hard he had to work those last few months when he went back.

He did it.

I was so proud of him as he walked across the stage in his blue gown, collecting his diploma from the tall man in the blue vest, who shook his hand vigorously. Uncle Billy's walk always had a dip and sway to it, as if he was dancing.

Afterward, a celebration party followed at their house. Grandma Baker, Addy, Aunt Nettie and I decorated with blue and yellow balloons, streamers, and signs. It sure looked festive. Family and friends gathered to celebrate this milestone that almost wasn't.

Unfortunately, Jerry made a fool of himself at Uncle Billy's party, drunk and angrily announcing, for some reason, to the entire gathering that he and my Mama hadn't been intimate in three weeks. Uncle Toad coaxed Jerry out of the house and took him home.

It was mortifying. Even for Uncle Billy, who is difficult to embarrass.

And Grandma Baker's reaction? She was proud of her son, angry at her daughter, and seething at Jerry's very name. Time with Mama and Jerry was becoming something that we simply wanted to survive. Nothing more.

On the night before our last day of eighth-grade, Mom asked me what I wanted. I screwed up all my courage and told her I wanted her to leave Jerry. I let go, just a little, mind you, and told her I thought Jerry was no good for her, that I thought she jumped in way too fast after Daddy. In my head, I screamed that she needed to quit drinking, because it was changing her into someone she wasn't. Could she hear it in my head? I hoped so. Because for some reason, I was afraid to say it out loud. And I pinned my hopes on the idea that her drinking was connected to Jerry and didn't really stick to her.

For the first time in a long time, she and I talked about something that really mattered.

And it seemed to me like she listened. It was the best gift she could have given.

On our last day at Graceford Grade School, Billy's anger surfaced again. This time Bean and I were much more to blame. Being on the other side of Uncle Billy's anger was no fun at all.

Seems another tradition in Graceford was to have a water balloon fight on the last day of school. We would have never known about this if not for Madari and Tommy cluing us in.

"It is classic, dudes," Tommy was explaining the week before the end of school. "Everybody hides water balloons. Once we're out, Graceford is a water balloon spectacle!"

"Look, pals, Tommy's right! You've never seen everyone get along so well! We all want to smash each other with balloons! It's so great!" Madari added.

Colorful, filled, wobbly water balloons were tucked all over on the outskirts of the school like contraband before the short school day began. Bean and I hid ours under the rocket-ship teeter-totter in the playground. We were ready for battle. We attended our essential thirty minutes, and then, school's out! School's Out! Teachers let the monkeys out!

Bean and I walked together to the front doors, nice as you please, and then took off like a couple of wild beasties to grab our ready weapons.

Arms full of colorful balloons, we launched them at our classmates, who launched right back at us. A magical event, insiders and outsiders, losers and rich kids all joined in this epic water balloon fight that traveled north like a soggy, wobbly mob until we reached Walnut Street in front of our crooked little displaced farmhouse.

Sadly, it was here that the water balloons ran out. The fun was over.

In a desperate move to extend the festivities, Tommy grabbed our water hose and began spraying in earnest. In a counter move, Madari and I headed into the house and grabbed empty pitchers from the kitchen, filled them with water, and snuck up on innocent attackers, dousing them from the back.

I'm embarrassed to admit this next part, but it's completely true. If stage one of the fight took place on the school grounds, and stage two on the streets of Graceford, and stage three in the Walker/Roadhouse yard, then stage four took place in the Walker/Roadhouse first floor.

At first, this development seemed too good to be true. Simone Schluter was in our house!

And laughing!

These kids hardly said boo to us at school. And here they were, grabbing drinking glasses, filling them with water, and throwing them at each other IN MY HOUSE!

It seemed so exciting. But slowly, reality flooded in. It got out of hand. So as enjoyment turned slowly to dread, we called off the dogs, even the popular ones, and sent them home until it was just Bean, Tommy, Madari, and me. We realized this had gone way, way too far. Inches of water stood everywhere.

Inside places soaked from Water Balloon Fight:

1. Living Room.
2. Bathroom
3. Kitchen.
4. Back porch.
5. Bottom stairs.

We spent the next few hours mopping, wringing, sweeping, squeezing, and shaking. Fortunately, it was a warm late spring day, so we brought a lot of items—hanging family photos, throw pillows, rugs—out to the yard to dry.

At last, in the early afternoon, when all of our drying tools were completely wet, we were finished. It was as good as it was going to get. The items in the yard were dry enough to put back in their original spots.

Madari and Tommy, exhausted, left, and we started to seriously consider taking a breath of relief.

Then Uncle Billy's pick-up truck pulled up.

He stepped in the in-town farmhouse, looked around, and adjusted his perfectly round glasses as a strange combination of 'whoa, I'm impressed' and 'hmm, I'm suspicious' crossed his face.

"Last day of school … and you guys have been … Um, cleaning?"

Since this was, technically possible, in chorus, we said, "Yes!" We were way too cheerful. We overplayed it.

Billy scanned the living room, and here's where our world seemed to flip, as it does in moments leading straight to misery, into slow motion. Billy turned to sit on our multi-striped tan sectional that all of a sudden looked darker than normal. At that moment, I realized we hadn't even sat on the sectional because we had been so busy sopping up water, and the cushions definitely looked dark, and wait, why were they so dark?

All the while, Billy was lowering himself down, talking about how wonderful it was to sleep until lunchtime. As his butt reached the cushions and his body, slight as it was, sunk down, water, visible water, began rising. It stopped at just above his waist. Meanwhile, the look on his face changed from boredom to absolute shock, and then quickly to fury, where it became stuck.

Without a word, except for Billy's under the breath mumbling, we went to work. Back to the yard we went with the couch cushions, then the big monster of the sectional itself, in separate pieces of course, Billy silently fuming all the while. Of course, there was no complaining.

The truth of it was our uncle felt responsible. This happened on his watch. You can bet there was shouting in his head. But on the outside, all we heard was muttering, quiet but sharp. By five o'clock, the tan monster was just damp. Good enough. We could surely come up with a plausible explanation for a damp couch. We brought it inside.

Billy left.

His parting words? "Inside the house? Seriously? Even I never had the guts."

The fight between Mama and Jerry that night had nothing to do with the out of control water fight.

"Maybe if you would have talked to me, I wouldn't have been talking to him. And we were only talking! I don't know why you have to lose your mind about it!" Mama's voice rose after the door slammed and they poured themselves inside, dragging their bitterness with them. It's all I heard before I sealed a pillow over my head.

Despite the conversation when I told Mama what I thought of her staying with Jerry, the two clung together, yelling, throwing ashtrays, drinking in silence in their separate corners, like this was any way to live.

Bean and I stayed away, usually upstairs, sometimes at Grandma Baker's house. The Cubs games were a great excuse, though batting away Grandma Baker's nosy questions grew tiresome.

Madari had taken to meeting me at church on Sunday mornings, allowing me to be sandwiched between her and Grandma Baker. I loved it. This particular Sunday, after the 4th of July, a hot steamy morning where you could wear the humidity like a hot coat of clouds, she sidled up next to me on the fourth pew from the front, where I always sat.

"Say, pally! You'll never guess wha—Whoa, buddy! What's that on your cheek?" she said in a half-whisper.

Fortunately, Grandma Baker was talking to someone sitting in the row behind us and hadn't heard.

Madari took her thumb and gently brushed across my right cheek, and I jumped. It really hurt. In more ways than one.

"Oh, that's nothing." I tried to laugh. It was utterly unconvincing.

"Nothing, my ass." She looked at the cross in the front of the church and told it sternly that she was not sorry. Then she linked her arm in mine and hauled me off, away from my Grandma and everyone, into the ladies' room in the basement.

"Look, I see fingerprints. Now tell me what happened." Then, she waited.

"My grandma is going to worry. It's nothing. Let's go back. See, church is starting!" I heard the organ music and started to get up.

I was afraid of this. Here came the tears. Now I couldn't go back in. I hadn't cried since it happened, and now I knew that, since my hot little soppy uninvited companions arrived they would be around a while.

Reluctantly, I began to explain to my dear friend.

The day before, we had gone to Mama and Jerry's friends, Rodney and Nance's, farm. They hosted a fourth of July celebration, and we were going to watch fireworks from the country on our way home.

Following the get together at the farm, as we headed out to watch the fireworks, I sat in the middle of the backseat of Rusty, with Newt on one side of me and Bean on the other. A cooler filled with beer sat under my feet in the back.

As we drove along, Mama called out my name. "Heidi," she hollered, her words thick and connected. "Grab me a beer from the cooler."

Now driving in a car with a drinking driver was nothing new for me. Maybe, let's see, about three out of ten times, the driver of the vehicle, to where I was heading, was at least drinking if not drunk. And Mama's hands weren't even on the steering wheel.

She was tucked up tight, holding on to her legs in the passenger seat.

Even so, I decided that I wasn't going to hand her a beer. If my mama wanted to drink, she was going to have to do something other than go through me.

"No, Mom," I said simply. It wasn't super loud, but she heard it alright.

"Now."

"No," I repeated.

My feet were on the cooler, so that is why this battle erupted between Mama and me. This was new and rare. I didn't often disagree, and never openly, with her. But I was not going to budge on this.

The top layer of reasoning was this, we were in a truck. She was an adult, partially in charge, at least of the kids, as this vehicle charged down the road. So, drinking while this was happening, was not a good idea. That was an argument worth making, I'd say.

But the true reason, the whole cake itself, was this. I was scared to death of her drinking. I was scared of her changes, of her need. I was not going to be the person who was going to just hand her the poison that she so casually asked for. Asked *me* for.

So, in that moment, I felt the risk like a solid rock in my chest. I stood firm, right up to Mama. I told her no, and would continue to do so, no matter what. I felt Newt and Bean supporting me.

In fact, both Bean and Newt moved their feet to the top of the cooler next to mine. I took it as a sign of solidarity.

Mama turned around. She looked at me with anger flaring in her eyes.

"Well, you little bitch." Mama pulled her hand back, and I closed my eyes and prepared myself for the hurt.

Like I said, I didn't cry when it happened. But with Madari's eyes looking into mine, determined to wait until I told her why I had a hand-shaped rose on my face, the hurt bloomed wide open.

Madari sat next to me and put her arms around me, tears covering her bare shoulder and the narrow strap of her summer dress.

"Mama," I said, like a wounded prayer. I didn't tell her that I hadn't said a word to Mama since it happened, or how I just sat in the truck and kept my eyes shut during the fireworks while the rest of the family sat on the rear of the pickup, watching the colored bursts. I didn't tell her, either, how Bean came and sat with me, his stinky arm butted against mine, saying that the fireworks were no good this year.

Madari didn't say a word. She held me until my tears stopped. More accurately, until our tears stopped.

As far as I know, Madari didn't tell anyone about the slap. Neither did I.

That week, we moved out, back to the upstairs storefront apartment.

We were selling our little farmhouse. Turns out the $2,000 for the house wasn't Mama's after all. It was Jerry's. Grandma was right. Mama and Jerry getting together shortly after we moved here was no coincidence.

The 'For Sale' sign in the front yard was heartbreaking. The only good thing about it was that we didn't have to see Jerry.

Now that we were back in the tiny upstairs apartment, I slept on the couch instead of in the bedroom with Mama. Bean and I spent a lot of time at the fort. We were delighted to find wild strawberries growing all over. We ate them until we felt sick.

Back in late June, a few thick bushes behind the fort stared budding with hard little green berries. We took one to Grandma Baker who said that by mid-July, the bush would be thick with blackberries. When they ripened, she promised to make us a pie.

We remembered. We filled a couple lunch-size paper bags with the tasty berries, popping as many into our mouths as we did the bags, and brought them to Grandma. True to her word, she transformed them into a pie. And it just might have been the best, sweetest delight I've ever eaten.

Bean and I ate it at her table, Addy joining us, one hot summer day. Grandma sat down with us with her own slice after cleaning up the baking dishes.

"Mmm. This is good. Hardly had to add any sugar at all," Grandma said after savoring a bite. She just held it in her mouth, enjoying the flavor. I followed suit.

We nodded our heads in agreement.

"Sometimes, even when everything seems out of sorts, you can still find sweet things in life. If you search," she ate another bite, then asked where we found these blackberries.

"Down the tracks. Little ways down from the house on Walnut," Bean shared.

"You found a treasure is what you did," Grandma answered. She was right.

Starting with our first discovery of this special place, our fort seemed about the only place Bean and I ever felt like we could talk.

We returned there on a particularly splendid sunny day, following a solid four-mile run.

"Do you think I'll be popular in high school?" I asked Bean.

"With those teeth? You'll be lucky if anyone talks to you." My eyes opened wide, the response he was looking for, and then he switched tactics, got serious. "Why in the world would you want to be popular?"

"What do you mean? Who doesn't want to be popular?"

Bean threw down the stick he had been snapping to tiny pieces. He leaned over and looked into my face. *Oh Jeez. Here we go,* I thought. *He's going to go all philosophical on me.* I set my listening status to maybe because I wasn't sure I wanted to hear what he was going to say.

"Popularity is like an illusion. A cloud you can't lean on. Smoke. It's meaningless on its own, but it can be dangerous. It has no substance. And to keep it, you have to please others, to keep making the ones you want to like you keep liking you. It's a game." He picked up the stick again. Started snapping. "Be someone others can respect. Then you don't have to get so tied up into what they think."

"You're popular, Bean." Now I am snapping a stick and flinging the little pieces. "You're a hypocrite."

"People don't mess with me because they know I don't care what they say. It would be a waste of their time to be mean to me, so they don't. You crumble. It makes people feel powerful to make you crumble. You aren't respected."

"That's not fair! You know I can't help who I am!"

"I'm not saying you can help it, Hide. I'm just saying it becomes part of how people see you. Makes you an easy target. You give other people too much importance. Care too much what they think."

He paused before he said this next part, obviously thinking carefully. "Hey Hide, your caring so much? It may be the hardest thing for you. But it is the very best thing about you."

My thanks got caught in my throat. A compliment from my brother was rare. And always genuine. I tucked it away.

The summertime blew by and the next thing we knew, it was the night before Bean's and my first day of high school. It didn't seem possible. But here we were, labeling our folders and notebooks, folding our cross-country practice clothes, and preparing for a new chapter. *What would this one hold?*

"I don't want you two to mess up your futures like I did. Make good choices," Mama said. How were we supposed to take this information? Grandma Baker told about her mom who used to stand by the sink, cigarette held loosely between her lips while her hands worked in the soapy water, saying, "Dotty. Don't smoke when you grow up," her cigarette bobbing up and down. "It's no good for you."

Mama's advice felt like this.

I sat by Madari on the bus as we made the six-mile trip to Adamsboro High School, where Mama, Daddy, and Jerry had gone to school. Where Uncle Billy had just graduated from. Where I would likely spend most of my days for four years. We were going from twenty-two people in our class to two-hundred and fifty. And the building was huge.

I was nervous.

Madari and I pulled out the schedules the school had sent and compared. Again. We had one class, English I, together right before lunch. That meant we could have lunch together, which was great.

"You know, Heidi, you can't just ditch me now that we are in high school. I mean, we're sticking together, right?"

"Wait, what? Umm … yeah. It's not like I've had a better friend. I mean, we're going to be running cross-country together and everything. You're stuck with me, pal."

"I'm sure that we'll have some other friends, too. But I really don't want to lose you."

I smiled, "I think we are pretty good, Madari."

"Cool. Just checking." And here, she broke out into a little song. "You've got a friend in me … You've got a friend in me …"

Next thing we knew, we were pouring out of the bus and headed to, well, who knows where.

Bean's and my locker were side by side, alphabetical, I guess. A.H.S. was like a maze. I arrived at my first class, Spanish I, in the West Wing by way of the East Wing and eventually a personal guide, a senior boy whose job was to do just that—pick up the lost stragglers and bring them to where they needed to be.

I was five minutes late. I don't know exactly if my teacher was happy or upset, because she talked to me in Spanish. But she smiled, asked my name, and went right on. I wasn't the latest one to class.

I was dizzy by the end of the day, wondering how long it would take for me to get used to this new place.

Madari and I changed clothes in the bathroom and went to the gym to meet for our first cross-country practice. Coach Quinn met us there. He introduced himself.

"Hey, I remember you from Sectionals last year. Heidi?" I nodded as we shook hands. He had a pretty good grip. "You ran a strong race. Just a few seconds from qualifying for state if I remember."

"Yes. My personal best." I was secretly thrilled that he remembered my race.

"Really glad to have you on the team. Your brother running cross-country this year?"

"He is."

"Great." He turned to Madari.

"Madari Swinford. I'm the best friend. She owes me big time," Madari told the coach.

He laughed. "So, do I. You won't be sorry, I promise. The others should be here any minute. Have a seat on the bleachers and we'll be starting soon."

We sat down. "Hey pal, did you see coach's calf muscles? Looks like he's got softballs in there!"

I looked and nodded my head. Madari continued. "And by the way, if we have to run, like, more than three miles today, you owe me a dozen chocolate chip cookies. If I live, that is. Seriously."

"If I can bake them at your house, you've got a deal."

Practice was the best part of my day. Running had become like a home to me. It brought me to a familiar place. And though most of the faces were new, Bean was on the team, and I loved that Madari was joining me. Since there were only three other girls, we were able to score as a team with five runners. And bonus? Her dad said he was willing to take us home from practice.

There were only so many ways to strategically find food without giving away our situation. Bean quickly got a job in the cafeteria so he could get free seconds after lunch. We went to Grandma Baker's about once a week without raising too much concern.

One Wednesday, while walking the hallway on the way to the cafeteria with Madari, who was sharing that a boy in her Algebra class let off what she called a 'boiled egg fart' five minutes before the bell rang every day, a bright orange sheet caught my attention.

STUDENTS, PLEASE COME SEE MS. SHEILA IF
YOU HAVE QUESTIONS ABOUT A.H.S. FOOD
PANTRY. ROOM 200.

When I stopped to read it, Madari looked at
me. "Everything okay, pal?"

"Just fine," I lied.

Ms. Sheila, I remembered, was the school social
worker. I made a mental note of the notice, but
even so, doubted that I would ever check it out. My
attention returned to Madari, who had returned to
her boiled-egg-farting classmate commentary.

It was not uncommon for the electricity to click
off in Graceford, so when it blinked dark on
Thursday morning, it seemed possible that it was a
short-lived, local problem. While Mama slept, I
went through the bills on the table. First, I found
Mama's check stub for work. For the week August
7–August 14, she only worked twenty hours.
Twenty hours! I found the power bill on the kitchen
table. Mama hadn't paid it since June.

I marched into Mama's room. It was dark.

Mama was hidden under her comforter. I pulled
it off, and she pulled the pillow over her head.

"Mama! Why are you only working twenty
hours a week? And why aren't you paying the bills?
What are you thinking?"

I heard a muffled response and grabbed the
pillow. Mama plopped herself partway up and just

looked at me. "You get to complain when you are a grown-up, Heidi. Until then, just lighten up." Then she grabbed her pillow back, covered her head, and closed her eyes.

Joy Roadhouse. Look at what you've become, my mind screamed, and once again she probably didn't hear, although I don't know how she couldn't. It was loud in my head. I threw the bill and stub on the bed and stomped into the living room, just in time to see Mrs. V. and one of the twins stroll past. Their faces both held small, secret smiles. *I bet your electricity is on, too.* I turned away. No ugly but welcome solace this time. As far as the Graceford joke? We held the lead.

With Jerry gone, Mama was spending time with her long-time friend Adele. In fact, she had pretty much taken over one of our kitchen chairs, the one with the piping cut in the top from report card day. This chair should have had Adele's name on it.

Later that evening, I sat in Mama's room and listened through the thin walls to Mama talking to her friend. I pictured them in their spots at the kitchen table.

"Joy, you may have to go to the shelter. It's going to get really cold this week."

"Please, Adele. Really?" Mama said, dismissing her friend. "It's August. It's not going to be cold. I get paid on Friday. We'll be fine. We've got plenty of blankets."

I moved away from the wall. The secrets were making us sick. I couldn't tell Grandma Baker or Aunt Nettie and Uncle Toad. I grabbed my notebook.

Why I will never be a parent:

1. Bills. Bills. Bills.
2. Insurance. What is that stuff? It makes no sense.
3. I will never be able to clean up someone else's poop. Or vomit.
4. How can a grownup take care of other people when they can't even take care of themselves?
5. There are too many brats in this world. (note: Simone Schluter)

With number five, I make myself laugh. My lists almost always soften me up. Maybe I'll keep writing them after all.

Adamsboro High School, it seems, has some of its own traditions. At the start of both fall and winter sports season, there is an event called 'Meet the Blue Bears.' The fall version happens on the first Friday of the first full week of school. Fall sports teams are introduced, and one-quarter of a football scrimmage takes place.

I was worried. I would be fine if my classmates never found out who my mother was, and I sure didn't want it to be the first week of school. I didn't want Mama to show up.

I decided to tell her that cross-country wouldn't be introduced at 'Meet the Blue Bears' this year.

"Heidi, I know the cross-country team is introduced. You don't want me to come?" she asked before I left this morning.

No. "I guess just come if you want. Supposed to rain, though. It'll probably be canceled anyway."

Mama's blue eyes looked up at me. She seemed hurt. "I get it. Embarrassed of your Ma." I thought of the Sectional track meet, of Mama running on the track. I thought of Mrs. V., walking through the streets.

My honest answer wouldn't come. "Mom, I gotta go." Normally, I would have said 'I love you,' but it was caught in my throat. *What am I? A coward?*

I rushed out the door, leaving Mama with her face buried in her hands.

It rained all day and was forecast into the evening. At the end of the day, cross-country practice was canceled, and Coach Quinn told us that 'Meet the Blue Bears' would be in the big gym.

"Be there by 5:50. Cross-country will be the first announced. See ya then."

On the way home, Madari offered a ride back to the school later, and I took her up on it. I had a bad feeling about it, though I didn't know why. I felt sure Mama wouldn't come. It's what I wanted. Completely.

When I got home from school, Buzz was gone. Mama must have gone to work for the afternoon, which was good. I did my homework, ate a bowl of tortilla chips with melted cheddar cheese, and waited at the window for our ride.

When Madari's dad pulled up in front of the apartment to pick us up, Mama still wasn't home. Now I felt unsure of whether to expect her at the school or not. Everything felt slippery; my stomach was doing flip-flops. Meanwhile, the rain continued to fall.

Since 'Meet the Blue Bears' was happening in the gym, a few changes had to be made to the activities, but cross-country would still be announced first, followed by volleyball, golf, marching band, then football.

I was feeling so nervous by this time, I just wanted it all over with. To be back home in our little upstairs apartment curled up in my thick throw that Grandma had given me.

"What's going on, Heidi?" Madari asked me, noticing my knee bouncing up and down. "You are shaking the bleachers."

"It's just, well, I'm afraid Mama is going to show up here and make a scene again."

"I thought you told her not to come?" Madari's face was a puzzle. I thought back to our conversation. I did, but not in so many words.

The cross-country team was announced, and those in the crowd who were paying attention clapped politely. Truthfully, most didn't even seem to know what was happening, which suited me just fine. When we got back to our seats, I felt so relieved that Mama wasn't here, which at the very same time, made me sad about how far we had fallen.

I wish I could have shared this moment with Uncle Billy, Grandma Baker, Nettie, and Toad. But I couldn't tell them without Mama finding out. Wanting to be here. It would have scratched at our family wounds. Our sick secrets.

We were broken.

After the volleyball players were announced, the varsity got to scrimmage against the junior varsity. There was so much going on in the gym that it was hard to pay attention to the game. Hundreds of conversations. Most people didn't come to see a volleyball match, and it wasn't holding many people's attention. I was thinking how great it would be to have some of their skills—serving, diving and sending balls straight into the air, when the attention shifted swiftly to the main doors in the entrance of the gym.

There was a skirmish going on outside of those doors, shadows dancing through the frosted glass, and screaming voices making their way through the door.

One voice, in particular, I recognized.

Jerry was here.

The door burst open, and there he stood, a madman amongst the crowd, searching for something. Someone. His hair was matted on one side and untamed on the other. His facial hair was scraggly. He looked like he hadn't showered in weeks. My stomach dropped. Madari grabbed my hand, and Bean, who had been sitting a few rows up, slid down next to me.

The volleyball players left the court, gathering in a tight circle around their coach.

"Look at him, Hide," Bean leaned in. Neither of us had seen Jerry for over a month. In the unkind light of the gymnasium, it was clear that this unkempt man before us, the one who hundreds of people were staring at, the one who was once an annoying but harmless and fun-loving person, was a desperate soul.

Jerry, scanning wildly, began to yell. "Heidi! Heidi Walker! Jeffery! I know you're here."

I felt eyes shift my way. Pretty soon, everyone, following craned necks and eye gazes, was looking to the area where Bean and I sat, and then to Jerry. Back and forth, like a tennis match.

A few people who I had seen at the school—the tall man in the blue vest who always looked friendly but serious, and an important looking woman—were trying to insert themselves between Jerry and wherever he might be going.

He spotted us and started heading our way.

"How dare you disreshpect your mother, you shpoiled brat! Get down here!" He sounded like he was gargling marbles. He had an old flannel shirt on. In his right hand, he held a metal water bottle. I knew it contained something besides water.

Coach Quinn moved ever so slowly in front of Bean and me, a human shield. Jerry continued to battle with the friendly man as the important woman held him back. "This is none of your business. It's a family matter," he yelled as the adults tried to reason with him.

"Shut the hell up and give me my kids. Heidi! Jeffery! Get over here now." The tall man stepped in front of Jerry. A quieter conversation ensued, the important woman nodding toward the bottle in Jerry's hand.

Then, with everyone in that gym watching, Jerry did something that replaced my embarrassment with panic. He rearranged the bottle so he could grasp it from the middle and then reared back, ready to toss it away, somewhere far.

He wouldn't, I thought.

Here stood my stepdad, in front of the whole school, a complete maniac.

"You want it? You got it," Jerry yelled, throwing the bottle high and away, as far as he could.

The silver container sailed through the air and hit a gym light which was surrounded by a wire cage. The light exploded, and the cage hit the ceiling, sending tiny pieces of white plaster floating to the ground.

In what looked like a dysfunctional snowstorm, the next few seconds went by like disjointed, slow motion movie scenes. I saw parents grabbing for their children and running toward the main door.

Mrs. Ford, my geometry teacher who stayed calm in every situation, guided people out of the gym like a flight attendant.

I saw Coach Quinn swooping toward Jeffery and me like a papa bird, leading us over by the stage, away from the crisis.

I saw my wild-eyed stepdad, who stole my mom away from me, wrestling himself away from the A.H.S. staff who were trying to protect us.

Meanwhile, a police officer burst through the gym doors.

Angry voices rose from the now nearly empty scene in the background, but I could not make out the words. The sound of my heartbeat drowned them out. *Please just let this be over,* rang through my head. I kept my eyes steady on Coach Quinn, who was nodding his head, repeating something to us. But as hard as I tried to concentrate, I couldn't make out a single word he was saying.

Suddenly, like another punch in the gut, I realized Mama wasn't here for any of this. And while I was glad she hadn't come to add to the embarrassment, I was also angry at her for bringing this desperate man into our lives, and then not being here to defend us from him when he lost his mind and his way.

When I heard Jerry's sobs, I knew it was over. I turned finally, to see him being escorted out of the gym, his voice remorseful and slurred.

"God, I'm so sorry. I don't know why. I don't know why," he cried.

Police officers, the friendly man, and the important-looking woman had their heads together.

I swore, in that moment, that I never wanted to lay eyes on Jerry Roadhouse again.

When Coach Quinn walked away to confer with the others, Jeffery leaned over toward me. "And where's Mama?"

I kicked my running shoe across the floor. "Who cares."

A Walker Trio Extra: Adventure #1 – Mama's Little Helper

Bean helps out.

Mama thinks we're taking a nap in our bedroom. Tippy-toeing softly into our room after an all-too-short nap herself, not wanting to wake us should we still be asleep, she comes upon this scene as she naively opens the door to our room. A pile of disposable diapers loosely stacked. Baby wipes spread randomly across the floor. A brand new but empty—How could that be; I just opened that tub this morning?—plastic tub of petroleum jelly strewn onto the floor.

Not good, she must have thought to herself.

Her gaze traveled to the bassinet itself. There she discovers a thin layer of white baby powder, lightly covering the edges of the scene, and coming together thickly to form a white blob in the center. A white blob with widely blinking eyes, naked—but who could tell—with a diaper very loosely attached slightly above my leg.

A proud Bean standing tall on a footstool next to my bassinet and grinning; a slightly sideways smile splitting his face, as if to say, proudly, "I did this all by myself!"

Poor Mama, who was expecting to find her babies napping sweetly in our room.

She reached the bassinet and attempted to lift me out. I, the blue-eyed, blinking blob squelched out of her hands. She tried again, and again I squelched away. Narrowing her eyes at Jeffery, who was getting the feeling that Mama just didn't appreciate his young genius, she said in a low and angry voice, "Get me a towel."

Five towels later, and an hour in the bathroom with hot shower running to soften and loosen the thick layer of petroleum jelly, my condition was upgraded from un-grabbable blob to slightly slick. Still dangerous in regard to being picked up, but manageable if one was especially cautious.

And there stood Bean, his sideways smile turned into a grimace, probably thinking, she just doesn't appreciate my help.

Chapter Eleven
Tequila Holiday

The Trouble with Parents:

1. They can repeat their own parents' mistakes.
2. They can change without taking you with them.
3. They are nothing more than imperfect humans.
4. They can marry an idiot, who is not your parent at all, but you have to claim him as one.
5. Nobody can hurt you more.

The rain fell softly as I waited for the bus for the second Friday of the school year, on which the first cross-country meet of the season was scheduled. Instinctively, I looked through my duffle bag, frantically realizing I hadn't packed my shorts. Now I'd have to run home quickly. But no, I mean, like a real sprinter, in order to get back before the bus filled with phone-loving fellow students.

Mama should be gone to work, so by the time I return home, duffle bag flopping against my back as I ran, I was confused when Buzz was still parked out front. I ran into the kitchen to find Mama and Adele at the table in their usual places. On the table with them were several glass bottles, golden liquid gleaming. I decided to have this conversation that I have no time for.

"Joy? What are you doing?" My voice was steady. Both she and her friend lowered their small glasses to the table.

"Heidi! What a surprise? What are you doing? Did you miss the bus?" Mama answered. Did anyone notice that I just called my mother by her first name? Because I did it without thinking. Mostly because I didn't really know who this woman was. Because she, in this moment, was not my Mama.

Because I could not stomach another disappointment from her. Right now, she was just, Joy.

And by now, I was sure to have missed the bus.

"I came home to get my cross-country shorts. But it's too late now, I'm sure." I think about being in school, where I should be. About my empty seat in Spanish. I feel guilty.

"Honey, I'm sorry. I'll take you in later. Hang out with us for a while."

"Why aren't you at work?"

Mama shrugged.

Their plan? Adele was going to teach Mama to do shots of tequila. And I, at my ripe old age of thirteen, was invited to join in.

Why did I do it? I like to tell myself that, when two adult women offer an opportunity to drink with them with seemingly no consequences, who wouldn't? But the answer to that question? Usually, me.

But I was so very tired of the fight. Of trying to bend the will of my Mama and get her to do what was right. I was defeated. So, I just settled into the moment. Let it be. I listened, and just like Mama, when Adele said pour some salt on the side of your hand, I did. When Adele said let the drink fall down your throat, I did. When Adele handed me the lime and told me to bite it, I did. Over and over again, I did.

I let myself fall in, to the place where Mama spent so much time. I allowed it to be my turn. This place was fuzzy and warm, and the world around didn't matter too much after a while. The fog continued when we got in Buzz and drove to a nearby town.

"I'm buzzed in Buzz," I repeated to myself as we drove along, watching the rows of tall corn. My head swirled, and I laughed at the bartender when she asked why I wasn't in school.

I was lost. Not hurt. Not happy. Just lost. Protected? No, not really. Hidden away? For the moment, for sure.

When Bean walked in that evening, his hair damp and uniform soggy from the first cross-country meet, which I missed, I was disgusted. With Mama. With myself. With Bean for not being able to save me from any of it.

"Jesus, Hide. How could you?" he asked with a look of disbelief and pity.

I wanted to ask about the meet, but I didn't deserve to know.

I had no answer for my brother. I was scared. I had ventured to a place that neither of us had been, and now I was alone, even though my brother was standing right next to me. We had been through everything together.

Until today.

Something had to change. This much was clear. Even if it started with Jerry, Mama had a problem of her own. And the three of us, Bean, Mama, and I had drifted apart. I was done depending on anyone.

My head swirling, I went into the room where Mama lay, either sleeping or passed out on her bed and dumped out my running bag. I put together what I thought I needed to be on my own. A toothbrush, toothpaste, a warm blanket, Harey, Bean's socks. I packed running clothes and wore my running shoes. I brought my school backpack. I hoped the rain had stopped because I decided the fort was where I was heading, and where I was going to stay.

Until something changed.

Until I figured it out.

Thankfully the rain had stopped.

Under the bright light of the stars, I stared through the fort's puzzle piece canopy, allowing myself to rise up into part of this beauty. Cleansing tears ran down the sides of my face, making the stars blurry.

My head was cradled by Harey, his silky pink ears catching my tears.

I fell asleep. When I woke briefly in the deep of the night, Bean lay close to me, the light orange cat sidled up to his chest. I picked up Harey, scooted him over just by Bean's shoulder, and closed my eyes, a slight smile on my face. Bean found me. I hadn't lost him.

My head began swimming again with the promise of sleep. Deep sleep this time. I fell into a dream, aware suddenly that I was swimming in an entire sea of tequila. I sealed my lips tight, knowing that I needed to get to the top to catch my breath, but I was drawn instead to a dark shape to my left. I swam toward it. As I got closer, I saw that it was Daddy, crouched against the side of the glass that we were trapped inside. He couldn't see me. He was looking straight through me, but when I touched his hand, we were back in our apartment in Evanston, sitting at our table and eating grilled cheese sandwiches.

"You're going to be a big star, someday, Heidi. You can really sing."

At that, I jumped on my chair and started singing one of our favorites.

"So what? I'm a rock star … I got my rock moves … and I don't need you."

Suddenly I started coughing, and Daddy started to float apart before my eyes. Frightened, I swam away, planning to go to the light, when I noticed shadows on the other side of the pool. I swam that way to see Mama, one hand holding on to Jerry and the other reaching out to me. I clasped her hand, intending to pull her with me, and as we touched, we were suddenly at Lincoln Park Zoo. I was four years old, cuddled up on Mama's lap. We were in the monkey house. I was fascinated by a young one in the corner who was flinging banana pieces at what looked to be a small friend, who ate the pieces as he picked them from the ground and his fur. The little monkey came to the glass and looked at Mama and me, and then went to her mama and jumped in her lap. I looked at Mama. "Did you see?" Mama nodded. I ached a little when I saw how much that mama monkey loved her little one, hugging it to her and picking carefully through its head fur. Every so often the mama would pop something into her mouth. Mama said that mama monkey was finding and eating tiny bugs from her baby's fur.

"Mama? That mama monkey, she loves her baby monkey?" I asked.

"Very much." Mama tousled my hair.

"Would you eat bugs out of my hair?"

Mama smiled. "Well, my little monkey, I'd pick them out for sure."

Suddenly, we were back in the tequila sea. I pulled hard on Mama's hand, but we were losing our grip. Our hands split apart. I had to get to the top, had to catch a breath. My head popped out of the liquid, and I knew I had to get out. I put my hands on the top of the opening, and pulled up, falling down the glass side of the huge bottle.

The fall woke me. I sat up in a sweat. Bean was gone, Harey and Bean's mysterious orange cat snuggled up by my side.

I knew what I needed to do. I didn't even need to write it down.

I gathered my things and headed down the tracks, straight toward the truth. My constant and demanding companion.

I knocked on the door of the parsonage, right next to the church. Reverend Jim came to the door.

"Heidi! What in the world! Is everything okay?" he ran a hand through his stick-up hair.

"Can I talk to you? It's important."

He looked up and down the street to see if I was alone. "Sure, yeah. Let me think. One minute. Okay, let me meet you in my office."

"I am not going home until Mama stops drinking." I sat across from Reverend Jim as we met in a cozy little office just off the sanctuary. One that I had never noticed before. I studied a framed sign that said, 'Let Go and Let God.'

"Mama has a problem, and I can't stay there until she stops."

Without asking too many questions, especially at first, Jim let me talk as he listened. He said alcoholism was like a disease, and that denial was an important part of it. Denial was a tricky character.

"You can't make your mom stop drinking. But you can tell her you want her to stop. You can absolutely tell her how you feel. There is an Alcoholics Anonymous meeting here at the church on Fridays at six."

"Here?" I asked. I didn't know that.

He also told me about the Recovery Room in Adamsboro, which hosted all sorts of meetings for addicts of all kinds. You can also get family counseling there if that's what your family needs.

I sat in the back of the sanctuary and took out my notebook, the words and guidance of Reverend Jim ringing strongly in my head.

And I wrote.

Why I want you to go to 30 A.A. meetings in 30 days:

1. Because your drinking has gotten out of control.
2. Because you are so sad all the time.
3. Because I want you to see me run a race while you are sober.
4. Because I don't want to stay in a shelter.
5. Because I need you.

Then I walked to our apartment. I marched upstairs, because without intensity in my step I might just stop and turn around. My head hurt, and my stomach hurt, and I knew I was going to have to say things that were really hard. Things I usually couldn't. I just didn't have anything to protect anymore. There was nothing to lose.

I flipped on the light, forgetting that the power was out, and sat on the side of her bed.

"Mom. I need to talk to you," I started. I watched her breathing change from under the comforter. She was awake now.

I gathered my courage and dove in, heart pounding, because the only way to do this was to start.

"Mom ... I need you to stop drinking. Completely. There is a meeting at the Methodist Church, right here in town, at six on Friday night, and lots more all around. Reverend Jim is willing to help you." I stopped and caught my breath. Mama remained still. I wanted to give her a minute to think about what I said. Then, I started again.

"I told Reverend Jim about our family, about your and Jerry's drinking." Here I paused again, not sure I wanted to continue. But I reminded myself that even though I didn't want to say any of this, I simply needed to.

"I am also telling Grandma Baker and Aunt Nettie what has been happening. And Grandpa Baker. I love you, Mom," I said, and then my breathing caught in even spurts as I inhaled. I blew out the next breath slowly and started again. "I really do love you. But ... I am not going to live this way." Here I surprisingly gained control. I was not a victim. I refused to be. Not anymore.

"I am done with secrets. Bean and I need to eat. I will not let you hit me because I won't give you a drink. Mom, you have a problem. Look for me at Grandma Baker's when you are ready to talk about it."

I tore the list out of my notebook, laid it on top of her still body, and walked to the door.

"Close my door," was the muffled reply to the reckoning of my heart. I pulled the door behind, walking away in so many ways. Maybe her response should have hurt me, but at least she had heard me.

I packed more things in my bag and walked to Aunt Nettie's and Uncle Toad's. Aunt Nettie was twisting Addy's hair into a French braid at the kitchen table.

"I need to talk to you," I said as I opened the door. I told her that Mom needed help. I spilled some of the secrets that had taken root in my soul. Pulled them out and laid them on the table like a handful of carrots, previously hidden but now in the open for the world to see.

Nettie, and even my sweet cousin Addy, listened. They hugged me when I left, my hair now in its own tight braid. Aunt Nettie thanked me for trusting her enough to talk to her. She said she wanted to call Grandma Baker but would wait for me to talk to her first.

My aunt did make me a promise. She said she would call Grandpa Baker, tell him what Mom was going through. We wanted him in on this, for Mom, and even for Jerry. He could help her learn how to battle her beast. We couldn't think of anyone who probably knew it better.

Next, I went to Grandma Baker's. I rang the doorbell and ignored the tune as I took a big breath. I lugged my big bag into the doorway, dropped it to the ground.

"Can I stay here, with you ... for a while?" I asked, knowing that this conversation was leading to a no man's land for us. At the fort, all alone last night, I realized it wasn't that I didn't have anyone. My secrets about our family was keeping me from those willing to be there for me.

That was about to end.

Imagine Grandma's surprise when I volunteered what had been happening inside the four walls at 110 South Walnut Street, her not having to ask the probing questions. Imagine her surprise when I said that it was Mom's drinking problems, not Jerry's, that concerned me the most. Imagine both of our surprise when I said that Uncle Billy had been the most responsible adult around our house in the past six months. His laugh reached us from around the corner.

"Uncle Billy? Where are you?" I called. "Get in here!"

He and Bean rounded the corner and joined us at the table. "Just sitting by the door listening to my amazing niece, that's where."

"So, can I stay?" I looked at Grandma, waiting.

"We?" added Bean.

Her arms wrapping around us, gathering us in, was her answer. In that moment, I noticed it. My own ship changed its direction. And Bean, once again, was by my side.

Interlude Two: The Decision

Joy Roadhouse stood at the door to room 116 at the Comfort Inn. It was September 4, 2017. She was stone cold sober, and she was a mess. Boney and pale, with puffy ink blue crescent moons under her eyes, blonde hair fried at its long ends, she knocked.

After a long minute, the door opened, and a tall, curly-headed man answered. A mix of emotions crossed his face until it settled on anger.

"What are you doing here?" Jerry asked Joy, who shuffled her feet. "Thought you never wanted to see me again."

Joy felt around in her purse and pulled out a small note from her daughter.

"I need to show you something." They walked into the room and sat on the edge of the bed.

When Jerry read the note, he burst into a fit of laughter.

"YOU? She thinks YOU are an alcoholic? Oh my God, Joy, what in the world do you think she thinks about me?"

The woman shot him a knowing look.

"Heidi's just thirteen, Joy. She doesn't know about life. Hey, and how did she come up with this '30 meetings in 30 days' shit?"

Joy explained that her daughter had talked to Reverend Jim, and her family, and was waiting at her mother's until Joy was ready to talk about it.

"I don't know, Jerry. Maybe this is what we need. Maybe. I mean, my Dad," she trailed off. Jerry moved closer and, taking a chance, put his arm around his soon to be ex-wife's shoulder.

"I don't know," he shook his head. "Maybe. Maybe we could give it a shot."

That night they drank themselves into a stupor, passing out together in the hotel room. The next morning, they decided together to at least try a meeting. Jerry volunteered to go with her— anything to be with her just a little longer. In the harsh but revealing light of the morning, going in a different direction seemed less of a joke and more of a ray of hope.

So later that day, at five p.m. on Tuesday, September 5, 2017, Joy and Jerry Roadhouse walked into the doors and were welcomed to their first A.A. meeting together. They sat around a long table in the Recovery Room, a small building in downtown Adamsboro, Illinois, as they heard their own story spoken from the mouths of complete strangers.

Just like these strangers, their lives had become unmanageable. Just like these strangers, they hoped beyond hope that someone, something, could restore them to sanity.

What Joy and Jerry discovered, together, was that they were in the right place.

A Walker Trio Extra: Adventure #2
Seeds of Misunderstanding

Mama, Bean and I sat at the dinner table one evening eating our hot tamales and drinking freshly squeezed lemonade when Jeffery asked Mama, "How long does it take for a baby to grow in a mommy's tummy?"

He was four.

"Nine months. About forty weeks. Why?"

"So, if baby seeds got in yesterday, when would that baby be borned?" Jeffery shoved half a tamale in his mouth, his eyes trained on Mama.

"Well, in nine months. Today's June 4th, so the baby would be born somewhere around March 4th. Why do you ask, Jeffery?"

"Shoot," said Bean around his tamale, ignoring Mama's question. "Your baby won't be here by Christmas, Heidi."

The sound of Mama dropping her fork, clanked loudly.

I looked at Mama's shocked face and went scared inside. Mama stood up and put her hands on the table. She spoke slowly but much too loudly. "What … Are … You … TALKING ABOUT?" Mama finally got Bean's attention.

I covered my ears with my hands, but I could still hear their words.

"The baby seed in Heidi's belly, Mama."

Mama breathed in and out, looking like she had seen a ghost. Her next words came out slow and loud.

"How? How did Heidi get a baby seed in her belly?"

"Just like you said, Mama. She eated the boy's seed. We want a little brother, don't we, Heidi?"

Mama and Bean looked and me, and I looked down at my lap. I had no words.

Mama walked out of the room. Bean looked at me. "Can I have your tamale, Heidi?"

I shoved my plate his way. I wasn't hungry anymore.

I didn't know that Mama would be mad about the baby. I waited for her to come back in while Bean cleared the tamales from existence.

But instead, Mama called me into her bedroom.

"Heidi," she was talking slow again, "What baby seed is Jeffery talking about."

"From the lemon," my voice was soft; my face hot and sweaty.

"Lemon? Did you say ..." Mama paused, "... lemon?"

I nodded my head yes. Mama wanted words, but nodding was the best I could manage.

Mama took my hand, and we went into the kitchen where Jeffery looked up. He was making a tower with the empty plates and cups.

Mama pulled me up on her lap where I could hear her heart beating. It was fast.

"Tell me about the lemon seeds, Jeffery."

"Oh, that," Bean said like it was of no consequence. "Bremember we made yummy lemonade yesterday, I asked if I could have some seeds. You said 'yes,' so I tooked three seeds. That made them my seeds. I'm a boy, so they were boy seeds.

"Then I found sissy, and I aksed her if she wants a brother, or maybe a sister, and she said 'okay.' She aksed me 'by Christmas?', and I said I didna know and would ask you. I gived her one of the seeds, telled her to eat it, and we would have a brother or sister pretty soon."

"You ate the seeds, Heidi?" Mama asked, and I nodded.

I held up one chubby finger.

"How many times have I told you that just because Jeffery tells you to do something, you don't have to do it?" Mama said, and I nodded.

Mama narrowed her eyes at Jeffery and stayed quiet as a mouse. She did the craziest thing then. She laughed and laughed. Mama laughed so hard that tears fell like rivers down her cheeks. Jeffery and I looked at each other, confused. What was so funny about a March baby?

Chapter Twelve

The Twelve Steps

Change:

1. You don't have to feel brave to act brave.
2. A bold move may create changes, some that seem awful at first, but be patient.
3. If you never take chances, you never grow.
4. Other people might see you different, sometimes good and sometimes bad. It doesn't really matter.
5. We all have power. Some of us discover it. Some never do.

Four days after I left the note on Mom's bed, I heard from her. She wanted to talk.

My ship was not the only one that had turned.

Have you ever rolled down a grassy hill longways? Spinning over and over so that when you stopped rolling, you were pretty dizzy and a little lost? I guess when you are heading downhill and need to stop and get back up again, it takes a little time and effort. That's how it was for our mixed-up, turned-around family. We were just beginning to head back up the hill, with some ways to go before we were where we needed to be. Maybe we didn't roll for too long. But we did pick up speed.

Mom and Jerry, though separated, went to meetings together just about every night. In the beginning, they just wanted to prove that smug Reverend Jim wrong.

But I was convinced that the preacher knew what he was talking about. I had seen the destruction of alcohol and drugs in Frank Walker's life. Not recently, but I had heard the story of Mom's daddy over and over. Did I really want to continue to see my own mother walk that path? No. I wrenched myself inside out to change this, to wish it away. It was a deep, never-ending hole for my energy; trying to get my Mom back to good. I'd been trying my whole life.

A frightening question lay in the back of my mind, showing itself from time to time, as she made steps to get better. *If I let Mom take care of herself, what good am I?*

The answer began to show itself when, on a Monday night, Mom rushed home from work and said that her new sponsor Julie told her to take Bean and me to our own meeting. They called this meeting Alateen, and she planned to take us that very night.

So now, she was blaming us for her drinking?

Bean and I rode in the back seat, both stone-faced and silent, on our journey to the Recovery Room. I felt my resistance churning mighty strong. I was getting used to the idea of them getting help for their drinking. But I sure didn't understand what any of this had to do with me. I was fine. In fact, I was more than fine. Call me Mighty Heidi!

The first thing I noticed when I walked into the building were the motivational signs on the wall. 'Be the best version of yourself,' 'Don't compare your beginning to somebody else's middle,' 'One day at a time.'

Corny.

We walked past a room full of laughing grownups who were about to start their meeting. I saw smiling, hugging, listening, nodding. It was cheesy and weird. They sure seemed like an unnaturally chipper group for a room filled with ex-drunks.

Then Mom walked us to a back room with about six teenagers and a grownup. The grownup, Mike, came up to Jeffery and me immediately and shook our hands.

"Welcome. So glad you found us," he said with a too-white toothy smile, deep dopey dimples, and a cheerful and sing-song voice.

I made a decision to go cold.

Be an ice cube, I told myself, determined to not let any of this warmth in. *What if it's a trick?* For inspiration, I imagined falling and dancing snowflakes.

I did not want to be here, and I wanted everyone who saw me, no, everybody who was even close to me, to know it. I imagined I was letting off a frost.

Mike handed me a cup of hot cocoa.

The meeting started with some readings. A boy named Shawn read that we were going to "share our experience, strength, and hope."

Um, not me, I decided. *I'm not sharing a thing.*

"What is said here stays here."

Easy for me. Not talking. Or listening for that matter.

"A family disease."

AARGH! Again, with the family disease. Don't they understand that it is my mom and stepdad who have the problem?

A girl with dark brown skin and, okay, hers were the most beautiful coffee-colored eyes I've ever seen, read a worn-out paper that listed something like the 12 Feet. Her name was Desiree, and I decided not to like her. I couldn't name the risk in liking her, but I knew it was strong. I stopped listening after step one, where they tried to say that I was powerless over the effects of alcohol. *Crazies! I am not the drinker here.*

I kept punching and counter-punching the words in my own mind while other readings took place. Then the meeting opened for discussion.

Desiree introduced herself. She said, "My name is Desiree, and I am the child of an alcoholic." When she spoke, I had to fight not to pay attention.

"Hi, Desiree," the others chimed all together.

I got a big lump in my throat. She said it just like, "Today is Monday," no big deal.

It glided off her lips like bubbles.

Do you remember the first time, and I mean the very first time, the idea came to you that you were, someday, going to be an adult? Like all of those dopey adults that surround you all the time? THAT'S going to happen to ME? It's a mind-blowing realization. Takes some getting used to.

So was this claiming, this announcement of sorts, that Desiree let fly.

A child of an alcoholic.

Oh no, I thought. *That's me.*

I can't explain how strongly this got to me. It felt like a punch to the gut.

Then Desiree started talking about her mom coming to pick her up at a friend's house while drunk. Despite myself, I lifted my eyes from the table, sipped my hot cocoa, and despite myself, my ears gobbled. Her words were like water, and I was a sponge. A big, hungry sponge.

She could have been talking about my life. Of course, she wasn't, but as this stranger talked, I started feeling like there was a connection between us so thick that you might actually be able to see it across the room.

She was saying things like 'detaching with love' and 'letting go and letting God.'

Then Shawn started talking about feelings, and stories that could have been from the mouths of Bean or me. Then Cassie talked. Then Gavin.

Thirty minutes into that meeting full of children of alcoholics, in the back of the Recovery Room, sitting there holding my half-full cup of hot cocoa, the fight inside me shifted on its axis. This angry tension I had been holding onto for a long while, probably since the day of my laundromat birthday, was called to the front of the class.

I noticed it, felt it pushing out from the tips of my long second toe to the top of my head. From the words of Desiree and Shawn, Gavin and Cassie, that could have been my own.

From the kindness.

From the connection.

And then, the melting of the cold hard shell I had been living with every day began. Warm salty drops streamed steadily down my cheeks as I realized Bean and I were not alone. I didn't say word one during that meeting. I didn't have to. I couldn't have felt more a part of this thing if I tried.

When I stood between Mike and Desiree, and they picked up my hands in theirs and said the Lord's Prayer, I felt the hard shell softening further.

It felt weird.

I felt the sadness and the anger start to loosen up; big chunks of ice exposed to warmth. I took a deep breath, not just a regular breath, but a deep, jagged one, a breath that would sustain more than just life, for what seemed like the first time in years.

After the meeting, Desiree and I talked for a little bit. She told me she was a junior at

Adamsboro High School, that she walked to these meetings by herself, and that she planned on going to med school to be a pediatrician someday.

God, did I believe her.

I said very little, but I don't think words at that point were as important as being. She put her arms around me, and I cried even more on the shoulder of her soft purple shirt.

"You are going to be just fine, Heidi. And remember this. You are enough."

I am enough? I repeated. God, did I want to believe that, too.

I replayed it over and over in my mind. *I am enough.*

Driving home, I was hit by this thought, here was this beautiful underdog. She had to be. Her life was a lot like mine. She had heartache after setback. And yet, she dared to dream.

Can underdogs dream? Should they?

"Mooommm, what's taking you so long? We're going to be late," I said, tossing her shoes toward her.

We were getting ready to go to the Monday night Alateen meeting, and I was more than impatient.

Mom laughed, "We'll be fine, Heidi. Looks like someone is looking forward to this." She grabbed her shoes, both of us a little surprised at this new development.

Twenty-five minutes later, sitting around a table that was somewhat like a home, I said it. If my words were a painting, this would not be a smooth and majestic watercolor someone would want to purchase. It would be jagged, with sharp edges and colors that didn't flow. But it was there, none the less. A different kind of beauty, I would realize later when I saw other members join, making the connection with the rest of us.

"Hi …" I stammered. My first word in the meeting itself. One of the hardest I've ever said. But I was going to keep going. "My name is Heidi, and … umm …"

I looked around. The eyes were kind and patient. 'Don't hurry,' they said. 'We'll be here.'

"Well, like I said. My name … and, well, my parents." I stopped. I couldn't do words in this meeting. No one judged. Their eyes were cheering me on.

"I am the child of an alcoholic." Then came the tears, mostly mine. A few from Desiree, but just because she was so happy I could say it. Mike beamed at me. Even goofball Shawn gave me a thumbs-up.

During my fourth meeting, I felt my story coming. The need to tell it was too strong, even though I would have kept it in if I'd felt I had the power.

You know the urge to vomit? Here it came. The story that I had been hiding from the world. The hurt that I had been determined to keep to myself. The damned truth. I came to depend on the support of this group of misfits, because together we shared a strength that alone we would never know.

"Hi. I'm Heidi, the child of an alcoholic. Many alcoholics, actually …" I started over, and I continued to tell them the story of my life, Bean's and my life, to this group who wanted to hear.

Bean came to some meetings, but not as many as I did. He had a lot more commitments on Monday nights. We were still close, but in a way, I felt like we were running in different directions. I was secretly proud of some of the things he was doing. He was in student council and was Treasurer of our freshman class. Even taking honors classes. It looked like Bean was going to make high honor roll.

A Walker-Roadhouse Family Extra: Steps of Courage

Me: Walking up those stairs to tell Mom I wasn't going to live like that anymore. If it wasn't the right thing to do, if I didn't know that in my bones, I would have run in any other direction than to Mama. But as hard as it was, I did it. Finally opened my mouth and let the words I needed to say rise out.

Bean: Stepping into the house on Evergreen Drive; believing we could live there one day.

Mom: Walking into her first meeting; admitting she would have to change everything before she lost everything.

Jerry: Walking into his first meeting, beside my mom, who we both love.

Chapter Thirteen

A Real Good Time

Things to say to a runner during a race:

1. Looking strong, (insert runner's name here.)
2. Way to go, (insert runner's name here.)
3. Strong and Steady (Uncle Billy's favorite.)
4. Looks like you are gaining on her!
5. Great finish! Run it in!

P.S. Things Not to say at a runner during a race (and these are especially true for non-coach people):

1. Don't let her catch you!
2. Faster! Run Faster!
3. Just a little bit further (when really, you've got a lot further)
4. Sprint!
5. Wait! You are still running?

The last week of October, Adamsboro hosted their one and only home cross-country meet. I was getting used to racing three full miles.

And I was especially excited about this meet.

One of my wishes was going to be fulfilled today. Mom, my sober Mom, was coming. Jerry was banned from all school events for the rest of the school year. I surprised myself by being a little sad about this. I kind of wanted him here. Grandma Baker, though, was still mighty angry at Jerry.

As a matter of fact, one day last week, Grandma stopped by to drop off pumpkins from her garden. She stepped in the front door and spied Jerry in the kitchen. Grandma, fresh off of bible study, scrunched up her nose, and then called out with no little irony, "Joy, Oh, Joy! I don't mean to interfere, darling, but I believe you need to take out your trash."

"Huh?" Mom turned toward her mother, confused.

"Well. It's just that some*THING* in your kitchen really stinks." Grandma sniffed the air, turned on her heel, and walked out the door.

After our warm-up, I saw them. Mom and Uncle Billy were huddled near the finish line.

"What do we do? Where do we watch from?" Mom asked, looking a little lost.

I pointed to the mile marker. "We cross the one and the two-mile markers right over there. This is where we finish. And Mom, don't tell me to run faster. When I'm going, I run as fast as I can."

"Well, I don't know what to say!" Mom answered.

"Help her, Billy," I smiled. He knew. I waved and ran to the start.

The boys and girls ran together; it was only a three team meet. I could see Bean while I was running. He looked strong. From a distance, I saw him pass the mile marker, our family there to cheer him on. I came a minute later and welcomed their encouragement. They beamed their support, and I soaked it in, turning it into energy for my race.

As we walked to Buzz after the race, Billy broke into a theatrical sports announcer voice, throwing his arms up. "Here we are, ladies and gentleman, ready to begin the 2024 Olympics. All eyes will be on the brother and sister team, Jeffery and Heidi Walker, as they both go for the gold in the 5,000-meter event."

"Anything else, Billy? Won't we be running the 1500 meter, too? Don't you believe in us?" Bean sounded hurt. He could act, too.

"Aw, sure. Maybe even the 10,000. Guess we will see, huh, Mighty Heidi?"

"Yep. I guess we will see."

It was nice to have them there.

We had come a long way.

Epilogue: Back to Joy

I stand on my tiptoes on the edge of the bed, straightening the tapestry, dark purple swirled designs against a light purple background, to the corner of the wall. It reminds me of the fields of purple bee balms at the forest preserve, where I love to go with Uncle Billy. Mom pulls up the corner and attaches it, the finishing touch, hanging on the north wall of my new bedroom in the beautiful home on Evergreen Drive that, a few months ago, I refused to get out of Buzz to come see. Last week, we painted. The walls are a light silver. Two bright white wicker chairs adorn the dormer space that looks out onto Evergreen Drive.

We moved into the house two weeks ago. I was wrong; Mom and Jerry found a way. Jerry was offered a promotion at his job at the University. Mom is back to work full time. I feel great comfort in being able to rely on them to be the grownups around here.

Well, starting to, anyway.

After Mom kisses my head and leaves, I just sit on my bed and look around. I can't believe this is my bedroom. But that isn't even the best part, which is that I have my mom back. I really wouldn't let myself believe it until now. I sit down on my new comforter and let it sink in.

I have my mom back, I repeat in my head. My scabs are healing. Turning into little scars. Scars that don't hurt.

Opening myself to the idea, I feel an anchoring to my own life that I cannot describe with words.

I straighten Harey the Bunny against the pillow, who also looks like he is taking it all in.

I used to have this 'every-day-a-new-life' theory. It went like this, every day we wake up a different person, with one particular set of memories for that, and only that, person. All we had to do was get through that day. Then the next day, we would be someone else, living a completely different and very possibly much better life. Part of me wonders if this might be happening now.

For the first time since I started wondering if this theory was possible, I hope it's not.

I close my eyes.

In this moment, I picture myself spinning, arms wide open, ready for life. My life. I know there will be times when I will have to draw in my arms to protect myself, from danger, or hurt, or cold. But this. This is how I want to live. Arms wide open. Free of my shell. Ready to feel the good.

I walk across the hallway into Bean's room. He is arranging his science kits on the built-in shelf across his wall.

On his bed, his new light orange cat stretches, a stretch so deep that his paws tremble. The large cat stands and walks to Bean's pillow, curls up in a ball and goes right back to sleep, covering his eyes with his paw. He's gone from wild to domesticated quickly. And the Bean and he have formed a solid partnership—the Bean has two soulmates now.

"Check this out," he says, looking a little disbelieving himself. "These shelves could hold a whole person and not fall. Want to go first?"

"Forget it," I say, and for some reason think back to an old experiment he liked to play, called 'Pull Heidi off a high place'—top bunk of a bunk bed, down the stairs, on a sled at high speed. I'd like to think I've wizened up to his experiments. "Maybe your cat can be your new assistant. I'm retiring."

Bean eyes the cat, who makes a statement by opening his eyes briefly, spinning around, and folding back into a tight circle. That cat is already smarter than me.

"Mom and Jerry are getting ready to head out to their meeting. I'm gonna bake some cookies? Want to help?"

"Let me finish arranging these first. Be down in a while," he said.

I go downstairs and pull out the cookie dough I made earlier from the fridge and begin to make cookies for the celebration that will take place here after the meeting. I think of Jerry and his desire to join people together, a meeter and a greeter, and am glad he still likes to do that sober. The other A.A. members, and those from the local Celebrate

Recovery groups that join in the social events, sure seem to enjoy it. This is the part of the program that talks about giving back. I am really proud of them.

Pretty soon Bean comes down the stairs and pinches out a sampling of dough. He pulls out a second baking sheet and starts to drop large balls of dough while biting down hard on a cold chocolate chip.

"Pretty good," he reports.

We put the trays in the working oven and set the timer. When I turn, I see a tiny bag with a large, hand-written tag, complete with neat, curly writing. 'To Heidi, From Jeffery, with love.'

"What's this?" I ask.

I knew by his look he was up to mischief. "You want to open it?"

"Sure," I answer. I take out the tissue paper on the top and reach and feel something soft. I pull out a pair of blue socks with the words A.H.S. Blue Bears on the side in white lettering.

"Thanks! These are nice. They might just be my new lucky socks!"

"Hope so," says Bean. "Student council was selling them. There's more," he nods at the bag.

I reach in the bottom of the bag, where I find a piece of cardstock. It is a note.

In the same neat, curly writing, it reads:

I, Jeffery Walker, forgive Heidi Walker her sock debt, totaling $492.14.

He had signed and dated it.

I am touched. "Wow. How come?"

"I was kind of a jerk about the socks. Sorry. I'd suggest you take that to your lawyer to make sure it's legal. I'd hate to have to take you for all you're worth in ten years."

"Thanks, Bean. I'll get right on that. But really, thanks for the socks. They're great."

Just then, Uncle Billy knocks and comes in the door.

"Hey Fruit Loops! What's cooking?"

"You're pretty late, but we can still use some help," I tell him. "You have class today?" I don't want to overdo it, but I am so proud Uncle Billy started at the Community College.

"Yep, just finished my creative writing class. My instructor is really funny. I have to write a 2,000-word story about a time when we broke a promise to ourselves. Your names may or may not be in my paper."

Uncle Billy helps us finish the cookies and other treats, just in time for Mom and the Cowboy-Hippy Jerry to return, opening their home once again. This time what they have to offer is hope.

This much seems certain. We will have to loosen the cloak of under-doggedness in our own lives. Stride for stride, it is being replaced by stability, and maybe even confidence. There has been great value in the struggle, great meaning in the fight. Among the strongest lessons learned was this, sometimes life can absolutely knock you down, or pull the rug out from under your feet. But as long as there is a chance, never give up hope.

And then there is this, when the underdog gets too strong, the title no longer fits.

I imagine that I will always, always, feel a connection to and love for the underdog. What is gone is the feeling of being stuck there, in that dark and shadowy world where struggle and fight, gloom and shame are the true center. The power belonging to someone else.

I think back to finding my own power.

I can picture myself going up those stairs to our apartment, seven months ago, to have a conversation that I desperately didn't want to have, but even more desperately needed to have. The day that I needed to tell Mom that I was done, that she could ruin her life, but she wasn't going to ruin mine. I think about how scared I was, but how I knew in my bones, it was the right thing to do. I risked it all. And no matter how it turned out, I could be proud that I was willing to take that chance. And the next time, when I need to shore up my courage and strength, I can think back to that day and remind myself that, no matter how hard, I was capable. I could do it. Risk taken.

At this moment, watching Mom and Jerry share their experience, strength, and hope with their friends, the world seems bigger and hope is strong. This is the creamy center. And it is good.

Heidi's Favorite Things about Me:

5. I love.
4. I am loved.
3. I know I am enough.
2. I know you are enough, too.
1. I am Heidi Walker.

Lisa L. Walsh

Lisa is a full-time school social worker, spending her days working to help her students understand that though life isn't always easy, the challenges make us strong, and that if we look for it, we will find good.

When not writing, napping, or trying to prevent teenagers from doing something they might live to regret, Lisa can be found running. As a life-long runner, she has passed the 60,000-mile mark.

Two cats graciously permit Lisa, her husband, and her two daughters to reside with them in Gifford, Illinois.

Reader's Guide

1. Why did Heidi refuse to get out of the car when her mom, Bean, and Jerry were looking at the new house on Evergreen Drive at the beginning of the book?

2. When the Walker Trio moved to Graceford, what would you imagine were some of their greatest hopes? Their greatest fears?

3. In their early years, before they moved to Graceford, their dad was in and out of their lives. How did this affect Heidi? How did it affect Bean?

4. Describe Heidi and Bean's relationship. How did the events of their family life affect their relationship?

5. From the first time she sees him, Heidi dislikes Jerry Roadhouse. What caused this strong dislike?

6. Like most relationships, Heidi's relationship with her Grandma Baker has a mix of qualities. What does Heidi admire about her Grandma Baker? Appreciate? What does she dislike?

7. How do you think it affected Heidi when she realized that her stepdad, Jerry, was not the only one to blame for their family's problems? How did that change her focus?

8. In the scene where the eighth-grade class is involved in shooting rubber bands and gets into trouble, why did Bean respond the way he did?

9. What was the importance of church attendance to Heidi?

10. What are some ways that Madari showed that she was a good friend to Heidi?

11. Why did Bean charge Heidi for wearing his socks?

12. How do you imagine Heidi and Bean felt when Jerry showed up at 'Meet the Blue Bears,' during their very first week at Adamsboro High School, drunk and out of control?

13. Alcoholism is often considered a family disease, affecting every family member. How was Heidi affected? How was the Bean affected?

14. Thinking about the scene where Heidi finally confronts her mother about her drinking; how did she arrive at that point?

15. Heidi's relationship with her mom changed throughout the story. As they move toward the future, what do you think it will take for their bond to continue to be strong?

16. Part of the lesson that Heidi was learning in her Alateen meetings was that she was important; she was enough. Why do you think that was so important for her to hear?

17. Who did Heidi depend on?

18. Who did the Bean depend on?

19. At the end of the book, Heidi explained her 'each day a new life theory.' Why do you think she made up that theory for herself? Why do you think, in the end, she said she no longer wanted it to be true?

A Note from the Publisher

Dear Reader,

Thank you for reading Lisa L. Walsh's young adult novel, *Hope ... Anyway.*

We feel the best way to show appreciation for an author is by leaving a review. You may do so on any of the following sites:

www.ZimbellHousePublishing.com

Goodreads.com

Amazon.com

Kindle.com

or your favorite retailer

❧

Join our mailing list to receive updates on new releases, discounts, bonus content, and other great books from:

Or visit us online to sign up at:

http://www.ZimbellHousePublishing.com

Helpful Resources:

If you, or someone else you know is seeking more information about Al-Anon or Alateen, please review this website for more information and local meeting sites:

https://al-anon.org/

Alcoholics Anonymous

https://www.aa.org/

Made in the USA
Middletown, DE
20 March 2019